THE CORPSE IN A CHESTER HOTEL

A NESTA GRIFFITHS MYSTERY

P. L. HANDLEY

CHAPTER 1

Nesta crossed the Grosvenor Bridge like a returning Roman Legionnaire. Granted she was driving a Citroën (as opposed to riding in on an elegant stallion), but there was something about entering a walled city that always gave her a rush of excitement.

She had not visited the historic city of Chester in many years and was pleased to discover that very little had changed (which was quite understandable for a place founded in the first century). Had it not been for her gift certificate towards a week in the most luxurious hotel she had ever stayed in, Nesta would probably never have had the excuse to return to this beautiful gem in the North West of England.

Crossing the Welsh border had become a rare occasion since her retirement, and it was now time to embrace the company of her English neighbours. Her only regret about this little getaway was not being able to bring a certain Jack Russell named Hari with her. *The Legion Hotel* had a strict "no pets" policy, and her loyal companion had to make do with another week in Mold, where he was to be reunited with her daughter's mischievous pair of cockapoos (something he did not take very kindly to).

Nesta was officially travelling solo and was already starting to miss her furry friend.

After crossing her beloved River Dee (the same river that flowed past her hometown of Bala), Nesta entered the city through its surrounding Roman walls and began the treacherous task of having to navigate Chester's busy central roads. Her usual driving routes involved little more than a zebra crossing or a t-junction, and she began to regret not taking her daughter's advice on working out the "sat-nav". Her map-reading skills had already begun to fail her, and, soon, she was circling the city centre like a confused hamster in an empty washing machine.

"Sorry!" she cried, after the second vehicle *honked* her. The idea of a one-way road system was an entirely alien concept to the woman from the hills of Gwynedd, and she found the whole situation almost as stressful as being stuck behind a tractor. "Yes, yes! Alright, keep your hair on! I'm from a whole different country..."

Once her adrenaline levels had finally started to subside, Nesta was relieved to come across a road that she recognised: Love Street. The name had stuck in her mind since first reading it on her gift certificate, and she hoped that her daughter hadn't secretly chosen a hotel in the middle of a thriving red light district. Thankfully, there was not a strip club in sight, and she drove down a street surrounded by gorgeous Cheshire brickwork. At the end of the road was an enormous hotel that caused Nesta to hit the brake pedal. She found it hard to resist gawking at this impressive façade with its Tudor architecture and black and white timber. It was as though the building had fallen from the sky and planted itself firmly into place.

The Legion Hotel had been entertaining its guests since the reign of Queen Victoria and possessed a presence that exuded charm and luxury. Nesta parked her car directly outside the main entrance and gazed up at the hotel's pointed, triangular roofs, which looked as though they might puncture the clouds hovering in the skies above. As she tried to take in her new accommodation, her concentration was broken by a gentle *knock.*

"Excuse me, madam," said a man in a traditional doorman's uniform. "You can't park here."

Nesta had been forced to wind her window down to get a proper look at the man's face. They were both a similar age, and he wore a long overcoat and a cap that almost covered his eyes.

"I think you'll find I'm a guest," Nesta called out. She could sense the man's snobby tone and was determined to milk her reservation.

The doorman took a step back to inspect her old Citroën and raised a cynical eyebrow. "Guest parking is that way," he said and pointed to a gate at the side of the hotel.

Nesta held her head up high and drove off down the narrow alleyway. When she reached the private car park, it was hard to ignore the expensive looking array of vehicles. There was everything from convertibles to enormous Range Rovers.

"You take no notice of them," said Nesta, patting her steering wheel in a bid to prevent her little Citroën from feeling self-conscious. "You're perfect just the way you are."

She heard the car croak, as she began to reverse into a tight parking space. After pulling her wheeled suitcase across a series of smooth cobbles, she approached the grand entrance with its marble steps and glass double doors. Nesta looked up at the canapé hanging above her head and failed to notice the doorman waiting for her.

"Can we take your bags," he said with a cough.

"Oh," said Nesta, pleasantly surprised. "How kind."

"Henry!" the man roared. A young porter came running

outside to answer his cry. He was barely out of his teens and wore a uniform that was far too big for his slender body.

"What is it?"

The older man pointed to Nesta's bags. Henry gave a disappointed nod and reluctantly began wrestling with the large suitcase.

"It has wheels, dear." The flustered young porter nodded and began dragging her luggage inside.

Nesta suddenly felt a little guilty whilst watching the man struggle. Malcolm tipped his hat and signalled for her to enter the hotel.

The reception area of *The Legion Hotel* made an even stronger impression on its latest guest than the outside façade. Its spacious lobby was lit up by an overhanging chandelier, which was larger than the one she had seen at Picton Hall. The polished, marble floors were as reflective as an ice skating rink and guests seemed to flow through as if it were perfectly normal.

"How the other half live," Nesta muttered to herself, as she made the long walk to the front counter.

The receptionist smiled at her and was stood behind her counter with the posture of a straightened squirrel.

"Good morning," said the young woman.

"Checking in, please!" Nesta was joined by an exhausted Henry, who rolled her suitcase to a halt. The skinny young man took a breath and scoffed. "Someone could have given me a hand. I don't know what that doorman thinks he does all day."

"Now, now, Henry." The receptionist gave the young porter a playful stare. "Remeber to respect your elders. Our guest doesn't want to hear you complaining."

"Don't mind me," said Nesta. "Permission to speak freely."

A nervous Henry ignored her chuckle and looked away.

"You're in room thirty-four," said the receptionist, lifting up a key card. She continued her usual check-in spiel and flagged down a passing young man in an immaculate suit. "Julian! Could you please see this guest to her room."

The young concierge had the dashing good looks of a Greek statue and a smile that could charm a hungry tiger.

"My pleasure," said Julian with a wink.

The Swedish receptionist was equally-blessed in the looks department and smiled back at him. Her physique was strong and athletic like a retired Olympian.

"Come along, Henry," the concierge called. "We'll take the lift and save your back."

"How generous," the reluctant porter muttered and followed Julian and his guest towards a nearby elevator.

Nesta waited for the steel doors to open before joining the other two inside. "What? No lift operator?" she asked with a laugh.

The two young men on either side of her seemed far too young to appreciate her attempt to lighten the mood, and she decided to remain quiet until they reached the third floor.

As she waited the entire ten seconds that it had taken for the lift doors to reopen, Nesta was a little disappointed at not having the opportunity to climb the beautiful spiral staircase that she had seen on the way in. There was something about ascending to her room whilst stepping on a red carpet that made her feel rather special (but that could wait until later).

She followed her confident guide down a long hallway full of doors and glanced at the metallic numbers whizzing by. It was hard to contemplate how many rooms *The Legion* had, but Nesta imagined it must have been hundreds.

With no windows in sight, the third floor hallway relied solely on artificial lighting, which gave it a never-ending feel that was absent of time and place.

They turned a corner and were approached by a guest that Nesta could have sworn she recognised.

"Morning, madam." Julian nodded at the woman in her elegant dress, who acted like he was an invisible spirit.

Nesta waited for the elderly woman to pass them and whispered to her guide: "Isn't that Debbie Backes?"

Julian nodded without turning around and continued his stroll. "We have a load of film crew people and actors staying."

Nesta clapped her hands. "How exciting!"

Debbie Backes had been a regular on her favourite soap opera for decades. Set in the heart of the Midlands, *Steeping Road* had been a big part of her weekday evenings since the sixties and Debbie Backes' character Appie — a pub landlord with a passion for flamboyant clothes — had been a permanent fixture since the beginning.

"What are they shooting?" Nesta asked.

The concierge shrugged. "Some film based on a book."

His guest sighed, having hoped for something a little more specific. "Any ideas on the genre?"

"It's not action," said Julian. "I can promise you that much. Most of the cast look like they'd be in *Downtown Abbey*."

"You mean *Downton*?"

"Mmh?"

"Never mind." Nesta tried to regain her excitement. "Sounds like a period drama of some kind."

"Sure," said the man in front. "If *that's* what you're into. Frida's apparently read the book. Says it's alright."

"Frida?"

"The woman on the front desk."

"Ah," said Nesta, noting it in the back of her head. It sounded like she would have better luck with Frida than this walking mound of muscle.

Julian appeared to be a person who spent more time down at the gym than buried in a book, and his broad shoulders made it hard to see where she was going. Hopefully, they would arrive soon, she thought.

"So what's Dame Debbie Backes like then?" Nesta asked.

"Is she a Dame?" Julian asked back.

Nesta shrugged. "If she's not, she should be — a national treasure like her." She could sense the man in front of her roll his eyes, even as she faced the back of his large head.

"I'd say *diva* is probably a better word," said Julian. "The woman thinks the sun shines out of her —" His professional instincts kicked in, and he stopped himself from saying anything further. This woman behind him was unlike any of *The Legion*'s other guests and had somehow caused him to lower his guard.

Either way, Nesta had got the message and was disappointed to hear about her actor's behaviour. "Never meet your heroes," she thought.

"Here we are," said Julian, stopping outside a door labelled thirty-four.

Henry had been lagging several feet behind them and eventually caught up.

Nesta entered her room like a child in a chocolate factory. Her eyes and mouth were equally as wide, and she twirled around to take everything in. "It's beautiful," she said.

Bright daylight poured through the enormous window overlooking Chester's rooftops, and the king-sized bed with fresh linen made her want to leap across its carefully-folded duvet.

The concierge had seen it all before and was keen to move on. He quickly ran through the list of amenities, which included an en-suite bathroom and a television with far too many features.

"Is there anything else I can get you?" asked Julian, whilst checking his watch.

Nesta turned to look at him and couldn't fathom what else

she could possibly need. "I think this will do just fine, thank you."

Once she had been left in her own company, Nesta headed over to the window and admired the view. Despite being surrounded with such luxury, she couldn't help but feel a certain degree of sadness. In her opinion, the room was far too big for one person, and she would have loved to share her little trip with someone else.

"Oh, Morgan," she said to herself. "You would have loved that bathroom." Her late husband had always enjoyed an en-suite, mainly so he could try out the free soap and shampoo. They had never been fortunate enough to stay in a hotel quite like The Legion, but that hadn't stopped them having the time of their lives. A free bar of *Imperial Leather* was enough of a thrill for Morgan, and they had never needed a television with more stations than the *London Underground*.

Nesta sat herself down on the bed and felt her initial excitement start to evaporate. A good bed and breakfast would have been enough, she thought with a sigh. The room suddenly felt much bigger and empty.

If there was one thing that cured a low mood, however, it was chocolate. Just as Nesta reached across the bed to grab the complimentary treat nestled on her pillow, she heard an enormous scream.

CHAPTER 2

The scream had come from the room next door, and Nesta didn't have to wait long to discover the source.

When she entered the hallway, the door to room thirty-five flew open, and a woman wrapped in a towel came running outside. "It's a *hand*!" she cried. "It's a *human hand*!"

Nesta had to rub her own eyes a few times to make sure that her vision was not deceiving her, for the woman in a state of sheer panic was none other than soap opera legend Debbie Backes.

"Somebody call the police!" Debbie roared, as other guests began to emerge from their rooms.

Nesta tried to move, but her entire body was initially frozen. She had never met a famous person before, and the idea of being star struck was now a sensation she completely understood. "Wait here," she said, having forced her stubborn feet to start moving, until they were making their way inside the hysterical woman's hotel room.

Debbie's room was even larger than her own (something she never would have thought possible five minutes ago), and yet, still, the actor had managed to fill every available space with suitcases full of belongings. There was even an entire mobile clothes rail, which contained some of the largest fur coats that Nesta had ever seen, including a costume that Debbie's character wore in Steeping Road.

Apart from the excessive amount of luggage, nothing appeared to be out of place (at least at first glance). Then, she saw it: lying on the pillow, like a complimentary item, was indeed a hand. Nesta took a few steps forward and saw that the hand was also severed. After another couple of steps, all became clear, and she breathed a sigh of relief.

"It's alright!" she called out. "False alarm!"

A weary Debbie Backes returned to her room and joined Nesta by the bed. The woman took her first proper look at what was clearly a prosthetic object and began to feel her blood boil.

"It's a prop," she muttered through gritted teeth.

"A very convincing one," said Nesta with a smile. "I could have sworn it was real. The fingers are so lifelike. Is it yours?"

Debbie turned to her with a furious scowl. "No, it most certainly *isn't* mine."

"The old hand on the pillow gag, eh?" asked a man in a dressing gown, who had appeared behind them to see what all the fuss was about. "I found a chocolate on mine."

Debbie turned around and glared at him. "You! This must have been *your* doing!"

The man's amused smile vanished, and he held up his hands at her. "Hey, don't look at me!"

"You're the prop master, aren't you? Surely you've seen this hand before!"

"It's one of my props, yeah, but I didn't put it there." He offered up his hand. "The name's Gary, by the way. We've only been working together for a whole week."

Debbie ignored his offer of a handshake and turned the

attention back on the hand. "Well, how else did it get there if it wasn't you? It's not a creature from *The Addams Family*."

"Thing," said Gary.

"What?!"

"The hand from *The Addams Family* was called *Thing*…"

"I don't care what it's called!" Debbie snapped. "I want to know why there's a severed hand on my pillow!"

"Someone must have stolen it from my props van." An amused smirk crept across his face. "You have to admit — it's quite a funny prank."

Debbie's eyes widened, and she looked as though she was about to sever a *real* body part. "*Funny*?! You think it's *funny* that someone crept into my room whilst I was in the shower?"

Gary shrugged. "It could have been worse."

"What do you mean it could have been *worse*?"

"It could have been a horse's head."

Before the prop master was about to lose his own head, Nesta decided to intervene. "I think what this gentleman is saying… is that, luckily, there's been no harm done."

Debbie stared at her. "It's harmful for my blood pressure." She headed over to her dressing table and grabbed a bottle of pills. "It scared the life out of me. I don't need that kind of stress at the moment. I've got an important job to do."

Nesta watched her pop some tablets in her mouth with the ease of someone who had done so a thousand times, and she swallowed them dry.

"I really love you in *Steeping Road*," Nesta said. "Appie is such a character."

The actor grimaced like she was swallowing another handful of pills. "Please don't remind me of that vile person. I'm glad to finally see the back of her."

Her words sent a chill down her fan's spine. "But… surely you don't mean —"

"They killed her off for good," Debbie snapped. "At long last. She dies in a pub explosion."

A shell-shocked Nesta tried to process the news. "That's not possible... I saw her on television, only the other day."

Debbie fetched a packet of cigarettes and prepared to light up. "It's not live television, dear. We filmed her last scenes months ago."

Nesta was forced to take a seat at the edge of her bed so that she could let it all sink in. "But... it's not possible. Who's going to run the pub?"

Before Debbie could remind her that *The Merryman Pub* was not actually a real pub, a smartly-dressed man with a sweaty forehead and circular glasses popped his head into the room. "Is everything alright?" he asked.

"Can people please stop coming into my room?" asked Debbie. "I'm not hosting a party!"

The nervous man pushed up his sliding glasses. "I'm the hotel manager, madam. I heard there was a disturbance."

"Well, *you* took your time. It's a good job there wasn't a maniac in my room! I'd be bludgeoned to death by now."

Elliott Ball, the hotel manager, was suddenly distracted by the hand on her pillow and let out a horrified gasp.

"It's alright," said Gary, marching over to his prop like a plumber inspecting a leak. "There's nothing to worry about. It's not a real one." He picked up the hand and dangled it in the direction of the hotel manager, who had to resist the urge to gag.

"You have to admit," said Nesta. "It *does* look pretty realistic."

Gary tipped his imaginary hat at her. "Why, thank you very much! I do try to get these things pretty accurate. You could say that I'm pretty handy!" He let out an enormous laugh which was met with a stone cold silence.

"Get that thing out of my sight!" Debbie roared, causing the prop master to scurry off out of the room with his treasured piece of prosthetic. The veteran actor set her sights on the squirming hotel manager and cornered him before he could leave. "I don't appreciate the level of security in this hotel. Do you know I've got valuables in this room?"

Elliott cleared his throat. "I can assure you, madam, these rooms are very secure. And you even have your very own safe." He pointed towards the steel container in the corner of the room. It was no bigger than a microwave and had a small keypad on the door.

"That old thing?" Debbie asked. "I could crack open a tin of cat food quicker than *that*. And if these rooms are so secure, then how did someone get inside to plant that thing on my pillow?"

The hotel manager was stumped on that one, and he began to mumble his way through a response. "I'll get our receptionist to issue you a brand-new key card immediately."

Debbie groaned. "Out! Everybody out! It's been a long night shoot, and I need to get some rest."

That explained why nobody was properly dressed, Nesta thought, and she began making her way back out into the hallway.

All the other doors had now shut, except for the one opposite. Standing in the open doorway was a tall, middle-aged woman with a sly grin and a mug of tea in her hand. She saw Nesta pause to look at her. "Did I miss all the excitement?" she asked, blowing on her hot drink.

"I'm afraid so," said Nesta.

"Shame. Let me guess — Debbie Backes? Such a drama queen, that one." The amused woman disappeared back into her room. She'd possessed a certain twinkle in her eye, and Nesta was pretty certain that the woman knew more than she was letting on.

All of a sudden, Nesta was craving a hot bath in her new en-suite and hoped for a much quieter soak than her neighbour had experienced. She headed back to her room with a smile. Never in a million years had she expected to have *Debbie Backes* as her neighbour, and something told her that her stay at The Legion was going to be far from a quiet one.

CHAPTER 3

After a long soak in her complimentary bubble bath, Nesta had decided to spend the rest of her afternoon exploring the streets of Chester city centre.

She started with a walk beneath the iconic Eastgate Clock before heading down to the two-tiered shopping galleries of Watergate Street. Stopping off for a short rest against the Chester Cross, she witnessed a performer dressed in a traditional town crier's uniform, who seemed to be competing with a human statue. Looking around at this busy junction, she felt as though she had been transported back to medieval England (although she presumed that there wasn't a *Costa* around back then).

The crowds of busy shoppers and tourists were always a little overwhelming for a person from the streets of Bala, but she managed to break away for a while with a stroll along the river side. By the time she had reached the racecourse, her feet were starting to get a little tender, and she sat herself down in the middle of the track. Fortunately, there were no horse races on that day, and she could be safe that a horde of competitive stallions weren't about to come galloping around the corner and trample her down.

Lying back against the grass, she could feel her stomach rumble, and, so, it was off to the cute little café she had spotted on Watergate Street.

Hidden away on a second-level Row, *The Sugar Spoon* café was the perfect place for a handmade sandwich and an artisan coffee. The Chester Rows were a unique set of structures built upon the ruins of Roman buildings. Now filled with shops, bars and cafés, there were still opportunities to come across various hidden crypts that only added to their mysterious quality.

Nesta climbed her way to the second-level walkway via a series of stone steps and was struck by the wonderful smell of coffee. She entered the café like a weary traveller who hadn't seen food or water in days and jumped on the last remaining empty table.

As she waited for her chicken and avocado sandwich to be made, her eyes fell upon a figure sitting in the window. Nesta enjoyed people-watching on any occasion, but when she saw someone that she recognised, it made the activity even more interesting.

The woman was fully engrossed in an old paperback and created a beautiful silhouette against the bright daylight coming in through the glass behind her. She reminded Nesta of a middle-aged Faye Dunaway and had been struck by her face when she had appeared in the doorway opposite Debbie Backes' room. The gentle sound of jazz music in the background only added to the woman's natural mystique, and Nesta waited until she had finished her coffee and sandwich before approaching.

"That's a good book you're reading," Nesta said, pretending to be heading out towards the door.

Jane Redman hated being interrupted when she was reading. She looked up at the older woman, who was creating a dark shadow over her frowning face.

"Sorry," she said. "I don't do autographs when I'm working."

Nesta was confused by at least two of the words Jane had used: autograph and working. First of all, she would never have deemed reading a book as "work". Secondly, a person had to be famous to warrant an autograph.

"Are you a singer?" Nesta asked. She received a cold stare.

If there was anything that Jane Redman found worse than being recognised, it was *not* being recognised. She was just about to ignore this annoying member of the public, when she paused to take another look at her face. "Wait, didn't I see you at the hotel?"

Nesta smiled. Now it was *her* turn to be recognised, and, unlike Jane, she didn't mind one bit. "Coming out of Debbie Backes' room?" That was a question she never thought she would ask.

Jane placed her book down and was suddenly intrigued. "Did you see what all the commotion was about?"

"Oh," said Nesta. "I saw *everything*."

The younger woman's face lit up, and she shoved an empty chair out with her foot. "How about you indulge me, and I'll buy you a coffee?"

Nesta didn't need to be asked twice for a free coffee and sat herself down at the table. She turned to point at the book on the table. The paperback was a murder mystery called: *The Shilling Murders*. Nesta had read the book when it was still high in the paperback charts and had enjoyed the Victorian London setting. The story had followed a female sleuth, as she tried to find out the identity of a serial killer who left behind a scratched shilling coin in the mouths of his (or her) victims.

"Are you enjoying it?" Nesta asked.

Jane sighed. "I've read it at least a dozen times."

"Wow," said Nesta. She had enjoyed the book but hadn't found it to be *that* good. "You must *really* be enjoying it."

Jane was starting to lose her patience but decided not to snap. "I'm studying the book for a film I'm doing."

"Ahhhh." Nesta nodded. The penny (or, in the book's case, the shilling) had finally dropped. "So you're acting in that Debbie Brackes film?"

The mere mention of her lead actor made Jane cringe. "Yes, the Debbie Backes film..." She shuddered.

Nesta clapped her hands. "How exciting for you! And who do you play?"

"One of the murder victims," Jane muttered through gritted teeth.

"I'm surprised I don't recognise you," said Nesta. "Have you done any films before?"

Jane hated that question, and she was asked it whenever the topic of her acting career came up. "I've done films, television, adverts, theatre, voice work... I've been working since I left drama school. Unfortunately, people don't recognise you unless you're the star of a soap opera or a lead in a successful drama series."

"Goodness," said Nesta, genuinely impressed. "Am I right in suspecting you mainly do supporting roles?"

"I've done everything — bit parts, walk-ons, one-liners. I've more than paid my dues. It's about time people recognised that."

Their table went silent for a moment, and Nesta was thrilled by the sight of her coffee arriving. "It must be very exciting being in a film with Debbie Backes, though. I'd happily be an extra in *Steeping Road*."

Jane scoffed. "Soaps are where actors go to die. Unless you're Debbie Brackes. She seems to go on forever. You can't be a good actor when your dialogue is churned out every week like a factory. The quality inevitably suffers. And I know Debbie agrees. She finds her whole career an embarrassment."

Nesta's jaw dropped. "She's embarrassed to be Appie from *Steeping Road*? Surely not."

"She absolutely despises the character. Debbie was a renowned theatre actor before she started in soaps. Her career is a cautionary tale for us actors. If you're not careful, you'll end up angry and bitter like her."

Nesta was keen to point out that she was sounding a little bitter herself but was more interested to still have her coffee paid for. "Well, she'll have plenty of time for other things now that her character has been killed off."

Jane stirred her coffee, staring into the milky foam with a sour face. "I think she'll struggle. She's been so typecast as a soap actor that most casting directors won't touch her. Not to mention the fact that she's got a reputation."

"Reputation?"

"For being difficult." Jane's mood lifted, suddenly. "She's known for being very high-maintenance and demanding. She got away with it on *Steeping Road*. Her character was so popular, they put up with her behaviour to maintain their ratings. But she's not a big fish anymore, and the film industry won't put up with any of that unless you're a Hollywood A-lister. Which Debbie is not — but thinks that she is."

Nesta thought back to Debbie Backes' outbursts in the hotel room. If her behaviour on set was anything like her attitude towards innocent hotel staff, it was easy to imagine her having a difficult reputation. "But she got the main part in *The Shilling Murders*?"

Jane rolled her eyes. "That's only because her nephew's the producer."

"Oh," said Nesta. "I see. That would help. I guess it's all about who you know in this world."

The actor in front of her nodded. "Some of us have to work extra hard to get where we want. I started my career knowing nobody. I had no connections whatsoever and had to work my way up from the gutter. My father was a farmer and my mother was a school teacher."

Nesta's eyes lit up. "Were they *really*? My father was a farmer. And I'm a retired teacher."

Jane's naturally-tense posture started to loosen. Her decades of working in a cut-throat industry had given her a hard shell, and she had worked hard to hide her working class background. When you had attended the type of drama school that Jane had, it was difficult not to feel like an imposter. Many of her peers had come from wealthy backgrounds and often well-known families. She had even managed to completely shed her native Lancashire accent in exchange for the Queen's English. She had been told that having a Received Pronunciation was vital to secure a role in the next *Royal Shakespeare Company* production and had taken the advice to heart.

But, despite all the scars from her intensive drama training, she had never forgotten her roots. Hearing about Nesta's background gave her a sudden warmth, like a loving care package from home.

"What subject did you teach?" Jane asked.

"English," said Nesta. "And, yes, before you mention it, I am indeed Welsh."

Jane smiled. "My mother taught in a primary school."

Nesta gave her a short salute. "She's a braver woman than me. I can teach Othello until the cows come home, but teaching children is a whole other ball game."

"She dedicated her whole life to that school," said Jane. "We lived in a small village, and she'd run afterschool clubs and all sorts. It was never-ending."

"What did she make of you wanting to become an actor?" asked Nesta.

Jane scoffed. "She was dead against it! I think she wanted me to become a teacher like her. Or at least have what she would deem a 'proper job'."

Nesta could see the sadness in her face. Something told her that Jane's mother might have still felt the same way. "I'm sure she was just being protective. I don't know many people who make a living from acting."

"Neither did she," said Jane. "I remember when I got my first bit part in a police drama, I was so excited to tell her."

"What was her reaction?"

Jane frowned. "She asked me who else was in it. There were some pretty big names from the television industry. But she didn't recognise any of them. She didn't really watch much telly unless *Gardener's World* was on. I told her it was a whole week of shooting, and she proceeded to tell me that the new supermarket near her was looking for a manager. She even offered to send me the application form."

The table fell silent for a moment, and Nesta could sense her pain. "You never know," she said. "You might land a role opposite Alan Titchmarsh in your next job."

Jane chuckled, and it had been the first sign of humour since Nesta had sat down.

"Yes," said Jane. "She'd be over the moon with that. I'd finally have made it."

Nesta leant against the table and gave her a mischievous smile. "Do you want to hear about all the drama in Debbie's hotel room?" she asked.

Jane gave her an appreciative nod and smiled back. "I would absolutely love that."

CHAPTER 4

Jane Redman had enjoyed every juicy morsel of info during Nesta's account of the "severed hand" incident. It was clear that Jane loathed her lead actor with a passion and was determined to savour every moment of her public humiliation. Once Nesta had finished indulging the woman with the final details of Debbie's horrified reaction, she made the short walk back to her hotel.

When she entered the lobby, it was hard to ignore the heated exchange going on at the reception desk, which involved a man dressed in a purple suit and a French beret on his head. Nesta wasn't normally one to pry on such a scene and tended to mind her own business (or so she told herself), but, on this occasion, she moved close enough so that she could hear the guest's loud cries.

"This is outrageous! I thought you were supposed to be a respectable hotel?"

Frida, the receptionist, remained calm behind her desk and appeared unfazed by this disgruntled guest's tirade of abuse. She had seen it all before and was more than familiar with *his* sort. "I'm sorry, sir, but our car park does clearly state 'at owner's risk'."

The man glared at her and looked as though his head was going to explode. "Are you trying to be clever with me?" he asked. "I don't know how they do things in Norway, but in England we have a thing called customer service."

"I'm from Sweden, sir." Frida took another deep breath. "And our customer service is very high."

The man's eyes widened, and he slammed his fist against the waiting bell. "That's enough of your bad attitude! What are you going to do about my car?"

"Any violence or abuse will not be tolerated, sir." Frida maintained her perfect posture and hadn't even flinched during the man's outburst. The guest on the opposite side of the desk may have had a temper, but he was a short and weedy man, whilst she was in strong, physical shape, having once deadlifted a hundred and twenty-three kilograms. She was certainly not afraid of *this* person.

"You call that violent?" asked the guest, pointing down at the bell. "We'll see what your manager has to say about this."

"I'm sure he would love to speak with you," said Frida. "But you'll have to wait until he's finished his break."

The man straightened his beret and stormed off with a loud *huff*.

"Are you alright?" Nesta asked, once the irate guest had disappeared through the main doors.

Frida smiled. "Never better. I love my job."

Nesta could already tell that his young woman from Sweden had a dry sense of humour, and, having witnessed the way she handled her angry guests, she liked her already. "What was the man's problem?"

The receptionist sighed. "Somone had keyed his car."

"How does he know it was keyed and not just scratched?"

Frida shrugged. "He must be used to people damaging his property. Seems like he must have a lot of friends. Great guy."

Nesta smiled. "Yes, he was wonderful."

"He's also a producer," Frida added. "Mr Felix Melvin."

"Is that right?" Nesta thought about what Jane had told her about Debbie Brackes' nephew. Judging by Felix's outspoken demeanour, it would make sense that they were both related. "Well," she continued, "I for one am quite happy with the service in this hotel. I think that the standards have been outstanding."

Frida smiled. "I certainly don't hear *that* very often. Normally, our guests come to me with all the bad news. We tend to attract the type of clientele who are never satisfied."

"Yes," said Nesta. "I'm getting that impression." She turned around and gazed around the lobby. There was a woman sitting beside an artificial plant with a guide to Chester's sightseeing tours. She was dressed for a day at the races, and her expression resembled that of someone trying to chew on a mouthful of ants.

Nesta turned back to the receptionist, who was busy staring at her screen.

"It must be exciting to have a film crew staying at the hotel, though," she said. "I can't imagine that happens very often."

Frida pulled her mind back into the room. "I don't watch a lot of movies." She lifted up a paperback that was hiding underneath her desk. "The book is always better anyway. I prefer the images in my head."

"Ah, yes." Nesta nodded. "The concierge mentioned that you've read *The Shilling Murders*."

Frida scoffed. "Julian told you that? I'd be surprised if he could even read. He spends more time focusing on muscle groups other than the one in his head."

Nesta was surprised to hear the young woman's harsh

opinion of her colleague, especially considering that she was clearly no stranger to the weight room herself. "Yes, he seemed like a person who takes good care of himself."

"Don't be fooled," said Frida. "Those muscles are all style over function. You ask him to lift a load of heavy suitcases, and he's sweating and panting after a couple of minutes."

"You seem to be very knowledgeable in that department," said Nesta. She looked over at the woman's broad shoulders. "Do you exercise much yourself?" Her question caused the receptionist to lower her head. "Not as much as I used to," said Frida. "I was a competitive weightlifter back in Sweden. My goal was to make the Olympic team, until I blew my knee out."

Nesta winced. "That's awful. I can imagine it must have been very painful."

"Not as much as being dropped from the Olympic team," Frida said with a laugh. "But I got over it." She raised up her arms. "Now, I'm living the dream."

"What brought you here to Chester?"

"I worked in hotels back in Sweden whilst I was competing." Frida smirked. "They let me use the gyms for free. Weightlifting doesn't exactly pay the big bucks, as you say in English."

"Your English is very good," said Nesta. "Although, it's my second language, too, after Welsh. So I'm not an expert." She paused for a moment to contemplate her own words. "But I was an English teacher my whole life. So maybe that does make me an expert. Hmh, who knows?"

Frida laughed. "I'd say that *definitely* makes you an expert. And I'll take it. Thanks."

"You were saying about your move here to England?"

"Oh, yes! So, I met this English chef in the hotel I was working at. He was a proper rebel type. A bit crazy, but I like that. Good chefs are always crazy. We became good friends. He moved back to England and started working here at *The Legion*. I was looking for a change, and he got me the job."

"And he still works here?"

Frida nodded. "You should try the hotel restaurant. His food is out of this world. Way too good for these people."

Nesta looked over at the doorway leading into the hotel dining room. "As a matter of fact," she said, "the hotel restaurant was already on my list. I'm planning to have dinner here tonight." She leant across the reception desk and whispered: "I get a fifty-percent discount with my gift certificate, you see. And free access to the gym and spa!"

"Nice!" said Frida. "Maybe I'll see you in the weight room."

Nesta balked. "Oh, I'm sure you will! I intend to make full use of my freebies. Even if it gives me a hernia!" She began walking away from the smiling receptionist, whose mood had lifted considerably since her encounter with Felix Melvin. Nesta had always enjoyed cheering people up, and (had her jokes not been as dire as a discounted Christmas cracker) she would have considered stand-up comedy a viable career option. Before she reached the elevator, Nesta called out across the lobby: "I look forward to giving my compliments to the chef! Tell him that there's a very hungry Welsh woman coming!"

"You won't regret it!" Frida called back. "His food is absolutely to die for!"

CHAPTER 5

Nesta wasn't usually a person who enjoyed getting dressed up. Generally, she much preferred to prioritise comfort over style, but whilst dining at a posh hotel, she presumed that her attire needed to be a little more formal than usual.

After a quick shower to refresh herself from the day's walking, she decided to forgo the elevator and make the short journey from her hotel room to the dining hall on foot. Descending the grand staircase in her favourite high heels was as satisfying as she had anticipated. Perhaps it was the red carpet beneath her feet, or the feel of that golden handrail against her fingertips — or, most likely, it was the surprised look that she received from Malcolm, who barely recognised Nesta in the dress she kept for special occasions.

The veteran doorman tipped his hat as she passed through the lobby, and Nesta half expected him to wolf whistle.

"Would you like a photo?" asked Nesta, who couldn't help but enjoy the attention. "You're lucky I'm back on the market."

Malcolm blushed and straightened his body as though he

were in a military lineup. A proud professional, he quickly looked away and pretended to mind his own business.

Frida sniggered behind her reception desk which only embarrassed the man even further.

Nesta entered the hotel restaurant with a slight degree of trepidation. It was far busier than she had expected, and the idea of a quiet dinner had quickly evaporated. She normally had no issues with a table for one, but the sight of so many groups and couples made her quite self-conscious all of a sudden. It didn't help that the last time she had got *this* dressed up for a meal was for her final wedding anniversary. Morgan had always insisted on eating out when celebrating their marriage, particularly at a nice restaurant. Gazing around the busy dining hall, Nesta began to realise that the rush of excitement she had experienced when getting ready was actually a bout of muscle memory from years of happy date nights.

"Are you joining anybody this evening, madam?" asked a waiter with a neatly-trimmed beard.

"Not tonight," said Nesta. "It's just me."

The waiter began leading her to an empty table on the other side of the restaurant, and she spotted Debbie Backes sitting opposite the producer she had seen earlier. Debbie's nephew, Felix, was boring his aunt with trivial production issues whilst she devoured her starter. He spoke with an intensity that reminded Nesta of an orchestral conductor, waving his arms around to emphasise his long list of problems.

"Over here!" cried a voice, as Nesta was flagged down by none other than Jane Redman. She was sharing a table with a man who appeared to have a complete disregard for dress codes and preferred to stick with his torn jeans and an AC/DC t-shirt.

"Care to join us?" Jane asked when Nesta approached. She pointed to the empty chair and had clearly consumed a few glasses of red wine, judging by the empty bottle on the table.

"Only if you're sure," said Nesta.

"Don't be silly," said the younger woman, as she turned to her male friend. "This is Rory — the only bearable man on this entire crew."

"Bearable," said Rory with a nod. "I'll take that."

Jane chuckled. "This woman grew up on a farm, too, Rory."

"Is that right?" asked Rory, shaking their guest's hand. "Welcome to the young farmer's club."

Nesta sat herself down. "It's been a long time since someone's used *that* word to describe me."

Rory swallowed the last of his wine glass. "Farmer?"

"Young," said Nesta.

Jane snorted out another laugh and clapped her hands. "I told you she was a good egg." She began trying to locate the waiter again. "Shall we get another bottle?"

"On a school night?" asked Rory.

Jane looked at him as though it was a stupid question. "Yeah, alright, then."

Once Nesta had been given her own glass of red wine, she took a long gaze around the busy room. "Am I right in thinking that most of these people are with the film crew?"

Rory turned around in his chair and let out a dismissive grunt. "I'd say *all* of them are. Cast *and* crew. The production is covering the hotel bill. We're all a bunch of cheapskates in this business."

"Some more than others," said Jane.

"So what is your role on this film?" Nesta asked the miserable-looking man beside her.

"First AD," Rory muttered.

"And what does that stand for?"

"First Assistant Director."

"Assistant *to* the director," said Jane with a cheeky smile.

Rory gave her a disapproving frown. "Don't listen to her. The

First AD is a head-of-department. He runs the entire set. It goes: Third AD, Second AD, Third AD."

"So he's the director's most important dogsbody," said Jane.

"That's not funny," said Rory. He ignored his tipsy friend and turned all of his attention on Nesta. "I'm the guy you can hear on set doing all the shouting. I deal with the crew; the director deals with the actors."

"You don't call action, though, do you?" Jane braced herself for a flying napkin.

"Without me," Rory continued, "that set would be chaos — put it that way."

Jane turned to Nesta with an amused grin. "As you can probably tell, Rory isn't a huge fan of our beloved director."

"Not a fan?" asked Rory. "I think he's an arrogant, pretentious, egotistical sociopath. Like most directors I've worked with." He turned around to glance at a tall, slender man sitting on his own table over in the distance. The film director had an enormous head of frizzy hair and a complexion that could only come with many nights of interrupted sleep. "As you can see, the great Victor is very popular."

"He's just jealous," said Jane. "Directors tend to be bursting with creativity, whilst the lighting and camera departments that Rory deals with is like working on a building site."

"Not true," Rory snapped with a playful grin. "I'll have you know that I'm also a skilled musician. Just because I don't walk around being all eccentric and cooky doesn't mean that I'm not creative." He pointed towards Victor. "That guy over there would be nothing without his crew. He just shouts *action* and stares at the monitor. We're the ones out there doing all the work. The cinematographer, the wardrobe people, set designers — once you've got everyone assembled, the filming takes care of itself. We don't need Woody Allen over there stumbling around pretending to do stuff. Anyone can do that. We might as well hire a chimpanzee." He swallowed a mouthful of wine. "But guess who gets all the credit? That so-called genius who calls himself a director. Or you actors! Half the time, the audience gives you lot the credit for everything. That's all they see."

Jane had waited patiently for the man to finish his rant. She had heard it all before. "I can assure you," she said. "I'm certainly not getting any of the credit on *this* film."

Rory caught her looking at Debbie Backes, who had already polished off the last of her appetisers. "Ah, yes. The star of the show herself. If this film is ever going to be a flop, it'll be down to her."

"What do you mean by that?" Nesta asked, rather defensively. Personally, she was looking forward to buying a cinema ticket to see *The Shilling Murders* (if not just to see her favourite soap actor on the big screen). Debbie Backes may not have been quite what Nesta had expected when meeting her in the flesh, but there was no denying her presence as an actor.

"She's been an absolute nightmare to work with," Rory continued. "We're behind on the shooting schedule, and we've gone *way* over budget — all thanks to her and that massive ego of hers. The entire crew are sick to death of her. This film might be just another acting gig to her, but this is our livelihood. Most of us work directly for the production company. If the film's a huge flop, we're all out of the job. A lot of us have got families to feed, and there she is acting like she's Scarlett O'Hara."

"Vivien Leigh," said Jane.

"Hey?"

"Scarlett O'Hara is the character. I think you mean she's behaving like Vivien Leigh."

Rory shrugged. "You know what I mean."

Nesta gazed down at the man's AC/DC t-shirt. "Are you a big heavy metal fan?"

"Whatever gave you that idea?" asked Jane.

"Don't listen to her," said Rory. "He straightened out his t-shirt. I got this on their 2001 tour. That was a great night. You know I used to be a roadie for Black Sabbath before I got into the film industry?"

"I'm sure she's not surprised," Jane muttered.

"You do look very strong," said Nesta. "Which I imagine you have to be when lifting all those speakers."

The other two laughed.

"Yeah," said Rory, jiggling his beer belly. "I suppose I do look quite beefy."

"What made you change careers?" asked Nesta.

Rory scoffed. "Ah, the film and music industries have a lot in common. People getting paid a lot for doing hardly anything. I had a mate who was a focus puller on *Gosford Park*. Got me a job as a production assistant. Then I worked my way up from there. My back was very grateful for it." He stretched out his arms and his neck cracked.

"I love that film," said Nesta, thinking about the 2001 classic. "Didn't it win some Oscars?"

"It sure did," said Rory, who began looking around the dining hall at various members of the cast and crew. "And it was all downhill from there. There'll be no Oscars for this film. I can tell you that for free. This is the smallest film I've worked on so far. Should have stayed in the music industry. At least I got free concert tickets."

Nesta let out a sly grin. "The last proper concert I attended was *Deathdemons*."

The man beside her almost choked on his drink. "You're kidding! Really?"

"I'm serious," said Nesta. "My friend from Bala is a big head-banger, and I tagged along to a gig in Wrexham."

Rory raised his glass. "Good on you! Keeping up the faith!"

He pulled out the devil horns sign with his hand, which she gladly reciprocated.

Just as they poured themselves another drink, the sound of smashing glass filled the entire hall. There was a unanimous gasp, as Debbie Backes fell from her chair in a state of panic.

"She's choking!" her nephew cried, running around the table to help her.

Debbie was now on her back, looking up at him with bulging eyes. Her throat had completely swollen up like an inflatable neck pillow, and Felix checked her plate of food and gave it a quick sniff. "There's peanuts in there! Some idiot's put peanuts in her mash!"

A crowd began to gather around them and watched him scramble for his aunt's handbag. He pulled out a yellow EpiPen before quickly administering a much needed shot of adrenaline.

"Call an ambulance!" a member of the spectators cried out. "For God's sake — *someone* call an ambulance!"

CHAPTER 6

Debbie Backes had been lucky. *Very* lucky. The shot of epinephrine had worked wonders, and, after some much needed medical attention from the paramedics, she was well enough to return to her room. There was no doubt that the cause of her rapid swelling had been at the hands of an unexpected dose of peanut powder, a subject that had got the entire dining hall talking for the rest of the evening.

"Everyone knows she's allergic," said a tired Rory, who had consumed far more wine than he had intended that night. The first assistant director was practically hanging off his chair by the time Jane had decided to retire to her room. He was one of the last remaining diners in the hall, and Nesta had been determined to stick around as long as she could. Her curiosity was getting the better of her (as it always did), and she had been making a careful mental note of all the faces present during Debbie Backes' dramatic collapse. These included many members of the cast and crew that she had yet to meet, but there was still plenty of time to change all that. *Someone* in that room had to know the real reason why Debbie had received a generous helping of peanut in her mash, and if it wasn't the fault of a careless chef, then this same person had almost committed a murder.

"Are you sure everyone knew?" asked Nesta.

"*Everyone*," said Rory. His speech had become quite slurred over the last few hours, which made it difficult for the person beside him to suck out every piece of information that she could. "We had to make it clear at the start of production so everyone was aware."

"Maybe there was a mix-up in the kitchen," said Nesta.

Rory shook his head. "A restaurant in this hotel doesn't make mistakes. Not with an allergy *that* serious. *Somebody* spiked her mash."

Nesta gazed around the room. There were only six people left, including Victor the director, who was still hiding in the corner, poring over his notes and storyboards. "Do you know the people still here?" she asked.

"Those three are from wardrobe, hair and makeup," said Rory, pointing at a group of women on the same table. Their plates were empty, and they had only just finished the last of their bottle of Prosecco.

"They don't seem too upset about Debbie," said Nesta.

Rory laughed. "Are you kidding? If there's anyone who has to put up with an actor's shenanigans the most, it's *those* departments. I can't imagine what it's like having to get *that* close and personal with a diva like Debbie. I'm surprised they're not drinking Champagne."

One person that Nesta *did* recognise was Gary, the prop master. Gary was sitting beside two younger crew members: Kris and Maddie. It turned out that Kris was the film's prize-winning cinematographer, whilst Maddie worked as a sound recordist.

"They're both a bit pretentious if you ask me," said Rory. Nesta *had* asked him and was intrigued to learn more. "Arty types, you know. Not long out of film school. Wait until they've done another ten years in this business. They'll soon get a wake-up call."

"Maddie must be the one that holds that huge stick in the air," said Nesta, as she pictured the fluffy object that reminded her of a feather duster.

"Boom," said Rory.

"Oh, did I get it right?"

"No, I mean, it's called a *boom*." He began mimicking holding up a long pole.

"Oh," said Nesta. She stared at these two young men talking away, presumably about the new wave of arthouse cinema. Gary was sitting in between them, sipping on his beer, whilst the conversation went straight over his head. "I bet that sound person hears a lot of interesting things." She casted her mind back to one of her favourite films, *The Conversation*.

"Oh, yeah." Rory nodded. "The sound department hears everything. Actors often forget that they're still wearing their radio mics half the time. I've heard some pretty funny stories."

Once the first assistant director had slurred his way through a handful of incoherent anecdotes, Nesta decided to excuse herself and wandered over to another table.

Victor Moore was still engrossed in his pile of notes when she approached, and the director hadn't even noticed her lurking over his shoulder.

"Those are very good," said Nesta, as she studied the pages of storyboards scattered across the table. "Did you draw them yourself?"

Victor pushed the curly hair up from his eyes and looked up at her. "Oh, uh, yes." The young director seemed annoyed to have been disturbed, but Nesta ignored the hint and took a seat.

"I wish I could draw like this," said Nesta. "I'm thinking of taking up landscape painting, you know?"

"Are you, really..." Victor had never been good at hiding his frustration and turned back to the comfort of his notes. He clutched his head as if it was about to fall off.

"But don't ask me to draw *people*. It's the hands, you see. I can never get them right." She rummaged through the pile of storyboards and found a scene that excited her. "Oh! I remember this bit. This is the killer's first victim."

A surprised Victor turned his tired eyes to glance in her direction. "Uh, yes. How did you know that?"

Nesta smiled. "I've read the book. And I have a good memory for detail. You know the victim was wearing a bonnet?"

The director frowned. "She was?" He grabbed a copy of the book and began flicking through the pages.

"Oh, yes. And I believe they found her lying face down. The shilling had fallen out of her mouth." She watched his enormous fingers, flicking through the paperback, which reminded her of the vampire Nosferatu.

Victor finished his dissection of the text and slammed the book shut. He sat back in his chair with a sigh. "You're right."

"I thought so," said Nesta. "We readers can get a bit fanatical about these things, especially when there's a film adaptation in the works. Although, personally speaking, I find the book is always better than the film — no matter how faithful the adaptation is."

The director began scrunching up the piece of paper in his hand. "Not with *this* film," Victor snapped. "I want to make a piece of work that transcends anything that a paperback can achieve. The book should never be better than the film! We filmmakers have a whole load of other tools at our disposal: sound, visuals, light, performances... watching a film should be a magical experience." He paused his rant and saw that the woman was just staring at him with a blank expression. "I'm sorry," he said, rubbing his enormous hair. "I didn't mean to snap. It's just... I'm under a lot of pressure on this film. I feel very strongly about making it something special."

"No need to apologise," said Nesta. "I would expect nothing less from an auteur like yourself. I'm sure you'll make a wonderful film."

Victor let out the first hint of a smile and nodded. "I appreciate the kind words. But, if I'm being really honest, the fate of this film does not look good. It's been nothing but chaos since the very beginning. Anything that can go wrong has gone wrong. I was beginning to think it's cursed. Now I've lost my leading actor."

"Who, Debbie?" Nesta placed a hand on his shoulder. "She's not dead, you know? It'll take more than a bit of peanut powder to take her down. They say she's recuperating in her room. She'll bounce back in no time. Don't you worry."

The director had never liked being touched, and his tightening body caused the woman beside him to remove her hand. "It won't make a difference," he said. "If the peanut allergy won't get her, it'll be something else. She was already struggling. I think the pressure's been too much for her. Debbie's been all over the place on this shoot. She's forgetting her lines, missing her marks, getting panic attacks —"

"Panic attacks?"

"Actor's have been known to get them from time to time. Usually the younger ones. Some of them party too hard and end up flailing during their takes. But not a veteran like Debbie."

"It could be her age," said Nesta. "We all get a bit wobbly as we get older and have our moments. Why actors don't retire like the rest of us, I'll never know."

Victor shook his head. He wasn't as convinced that Debbie Backes might have just been showing her age. He had worked with several performers who were older than her, and they could perfectly hold their own with the younger talent (if anything, they often stole the show). "Many actors do their best work as they get older," he said. "I've known many who barely got auditions in their youth from all the competition. Then, all of a sudden, the pool of available talent grows smaller, and they're rewarded for sticking it out." The director picked up the book and sighed. "I don't know... maybe this'll end up being my Don Quixote."

"Like the opera?" Nesta asked.

"I'm talking about the troubled history of bringing the character to the screen," said Victor. "Terry Gilliam spent half of his life trying to make that film. Orson Welles even tried but failed."

Nesta was beginning to see what his drunken assistant director had meant. Victor really *did* think he was making Citizen Kane, she thought (and he was certainly not as funny as a former Monty Python member). "You're still young," she said. "There's plenty of time."

"Not if this film kills me first," said Victor. His choice of words disturbed his listener, who assumed that he was joking.

"I'm sure you don't mean that," she said.

"No? Everything that *can* go wrong *has* gone wrong. We've had bad weather, faulty props, malfunctioning equipment, incompetent actors. None of my crew members seem to care." Victor picked up a page of storyboards and waved it at her. "You were talking about attention to detail earlier? Nobody on this production has any of that. They're acting like we're making some TV special."

A weary Nesta tried to humour him with a nod. It seemed that there was no helping this troubled man and his precious vision. Or was there? "You know what you need to do, Victor?" Nesta stood up and had his full attention. He glared at her in the hope that she could finally give him the answer to all of his problems. She leant forward and smiled. "You need to have a nice cup of tea and get a good night's sleep." The director's face fell with bitter disappointment, and he squirmed as the hand returned to his shoulder.

"You really need to be more positive with these things," Nesta continued, tapping him on the arm. "Cheer up, lad. After all — it's not like anyone's died or anything!"

CHAPTER 7

Nesta was normally an early riser, but, seeing as she had experienced an unexpected late night of socialising during the aftermath of the peanut mash incident, her first morning at *The Legion Hotel* had started at around ten o'clock.

The breakfast buffet had come as a welcome sight, and Nesta enjoyed nothing more than cramming her plate full of a wide selection of sweet and savoury items. Only in a hotel would she ever have contemplated a full English breakfast with extra sides of fruit, pastries and three different types of yoghurt. On a regular day at home, she would have been quite happy with a cup of Yorkshire, and yet, that morning, Nesta had decided to have a coffee, a tea, two smoothies and a glass of orange juice. *That* would be a sufficient start to the day, her holiday brain thought.

After going back up for seconds, she noticed a depressed-looking individual sitting in the corner of the dining hall. The man dressed in chef whites was sipping on a large mug of coffee and didn't even notice her approaching.

"Are you one of the chefs here?" she asked. Her stomach was

already struggling with the overload of food, and she was almost tempted to go straight back to bed.

"I'm the head chef." The man uttered his job title as though he were embarrassed to mention it.

"Ah! You must be Frida's friend."

The man known as Billy raised his head to look at her. "How do you know Frida?"

"We only just met," said Nesta. "I arrived yesterday, and she recommended your restaurant."

The disappointed chef nodded. "How good of her."

"I wanted to send my compliments after a wonderful meal last night." Nesta let out a chef's kiss.

Billy scoffed. "I'm glad *someone* enjoyed it. Unlike that poor woman."

Nesta nodded. "Yes... I suppose not all of us were entirely satisfied. But everyone makes mistakes." Her careful choice of words were followed by a pause, as she waited for the reaction.

"*Mistake*?" Billy asked. He glared at her with a trembling lip. "I never make mistakes when it comes to food."

"But —"

"I know what you're referring to," Billy snapped. "And I've been lying awake all night thinking about it. However that peanut powder got into the mash, it had nothing to do with me or my team. We're very careful when it comes to food allergies. It's not something you can get away with very easily."

"I'm sure you were extremely careful," said Nesta. "But, sometimes —"

"It was not a mistake," said the stern chef. "That mash was perfect when it left the hotplate. Whatever happens to it after that is out of my control."

Nesta didn't think that the man's mood could darken any further, but she was proven wrong. "Are you suggesting that someone spiked her mash?" she asked. "*After* it had left the kitchen?"

"Unless Mrs Backes garnished that plate herself with a full bottle of peanut powder, somebody else did it for her. I plated it up myself."

"Was there anyone else in that kitchen that shouldn't have been?"

"There was nobody but the staff," Billy snapped. "I run a tight ship. No one enters my kitchen without permission, especially not members of the public."

Nesta stroked her chin and gazed around the dining hall. "Interesting. So it must have been tampered with after leaving the kitchen."

Billy swallowed another mouthful of coffee. "I never send a plate out that I'm not happy with — ever! I make a point to inspect every meal on that hot plate before it goes out. Any head chef worth their salt would do the same. It's bad enough that we have to hand over something so perfect to a bunch of mindless waiting staff."

"You don't trust the front of house staff?" Nesta asked. She caught a glimpse of the bearded waiter that she had seen the night before, who was busy chuckling beside one of the waitresses.

Billy grimaced. "I never trust the waiting staff. They're all the same. Wherever I've worked, someone always manages to mess something up. It's usually just a matter of time. They just don't have that same level of passion that we do. I actually care about how my food arrives at the customer's table. The servers will quite happily just let it go cold before they take it out. It drives me mad. But what do you expect when you get kids and students to do that job. It's just a stop gap to them. But this is my whole life."

Nesta listened with great fascination. She had never been

much of a chef when preparing her home cooked meals. As long as it was cooked and edible, the meal was good enough for her. Perhaps, in future, she might take more pride in her signature scrambled eggs on toast. "That waiter doesn't look too young," she said, pointing at the man with the fabulous beard.

The chef scoffed. "Some of the young waiting staff just get older. That doesn't mean that their mindset has changed — or their work ethic. Leigh's been here since he was a student. He just never left. Useless, flaming hipster. It's about time the guy grew up and took his job more seriously."

Leigh's laugh echoed around the dining hall, which only infuriated the head chef even more.

"What did he study?" Nesta asked.

Billy looked up at her in disgust. "Why should I care? Probably a degree in coffee-making. Everyone thinks they're a chef nowadays, even café workers."

Nesta was starting to see why Billy was normally hidden away in the kitchen. Despite his disdain for waiters, he didn't exactly possess the people-skills to perform the job himself, and she had deduced that it was probably best that he remained in the kitchen (for everyone's sake).

HAVING SCHMOOZED her way through various members of the resident film crew, Nesta had picked up a rather interesting tip-off regarding the production's shooting schedule. It had turned out that the shoot was grossly behind on its ongoing night shoots, and, therefore, Victor had been forced to make a compromise on one of his favourite scenes.

"We're shooting day for night," had been the words of his first assistant director. Or was it "night for day?" Nesta asked herself. Either way, the shoot was due to take place that morning in a location that Nesta had been keen to visit.

The Roman Gardens was a small park that showcased a handful of ruins from the legionary fortress of Deva. Located on Pepper Street with a central path leading down to the river, the gardens were the perfect setting for a private meeting between two characters in a dramatic story — like a film called *The Shilling Murders*.

Only a short walk from the hotel, the gardens had been an easy place to get to. Getting in, however, was an entirely different story. It wasn't every day that a big film production was in town, and the entrance on Pepper Street was blocked off by a crowd of curious spectators. The road itself had been temporarily closed, and the pavements were lined with a series of large production vehicles.

Nesta had hoped that she could stroll straight onto set like a lead actor, but, instead, was forced to stand on her tip toes just to get a glimpse of what was happening.

"I'm going to have to ask you all to move back," said a burly security guard, as he tried to make room for an enormous light to be wheeled through the entrance.

Once the crowd had parted, Nesta decided to make her move and darted through like a determined wasp.

"Madam! Stop right there!"

Nesta froze, as the security guard began towering over her.

"You can't go in there," the man said with his deep voice.

"Oh," said Nesta, smiling and fluttering her eyelashes. "It's okay. I'm with the film crew."

The security guard folded up his arms and raised an eyebrow. "Oh, aye? Then where's your pass, love?"

Nesta hated it when people called her "love" but gritted her teeth and forced out an even bigger smile. When she began stuttering, the man pointed towards the crowd of pedestrians. "Out — now!"

The security guard waited for her to move but saw that she was distracted by something behind him.

"Hello!" Nesta called out, whilst waving frantically. The large man in front of her turned around to see Rory, the first assistant director, signalling for her to head over.

Nesta smiled. "I'm afraid I'm going to have to ask you to move aside now," she said and waited for the stunned security guard to move out of her way.

"Uh, yeah, sure thing. I didn't realise —"

Nesta could still hear the man's stuttering long after she had walked away and made the short walk towards the set. Her head was now held up high, as she passed various crew members with large pieces of props and filming equipment.

"I've got a bone to pick with you," said Rory, as she approached. His eyes were bloodshot, and he had the complexion of someone with a severe hangover. "Why did you buy me that extra bottle? You should have stopped me after the first couple."

"I have no idea what you're talking about," said Nesta with an innocent smile. She had known the key to this man's heart, and it came in the form of Pinot Noir. It hadn't taken long to realise that Rory had very loose lips after a few glasses of his favourite drink, and she had learnt a great deal about the troubled production of *The Shilling Murders*. "I think you must have had too much to drink. Your memory's a little hazy."

Rory gave her a suspicious stare and checked her watch. "We're so behind," he muttered. "Did you see Jane or Debbie when you left the hotel?"

Nesta shook her head and couldn't believe that she was now on first-name terms with an actor like Debbie Backes (not that the woman herself would remember who she was). "To be fair," she said, "Debbie *did* come close to choking to death last night. I would be surprised if she's feeling like shooting a scene today."

"She doesn't have a choice," Rory snapped. "There's too much at stake for her not to perform. She'll be here. I just hope it's within the next hour."

"I'm surprised that Jane's not here," said Nesta, looking around. "She seemed very prepared."

"She's also a lightweight," Rory muttered. He couldn't help but feel guilty about topping up her glass a few times the night before. "We've worked on a few jobs together over the years. One glass of wine, and she's plastered. Our last wrap party ended with her wrestling down one of the producers. She says she has three brothers."

They both turned to see the person in question making their way through into the gardens. Jane Redman was hiding her eyes behind a large pair of sunglasses and walked as though she was an extra in *The Night of the Living Dead*.

"Jane!" Rory cried out.

The actor saw him and shuddered. She would rather have been tucked up underneath her bed sheets at that very moment and could feel her body wanting to vomit.

"You took your time," said Rory. "How are we? Fresh as a daisy?"

Jane gave him an unamused scowl. "I don't see why you're so worried about me," she said. "I'm playing a corpse today, remember? I hardly need to be fresh to lie down in the grass and play dead."

"Oh!" Nesta cried, clapping her hands. "Yes, I remember — this is the scene where they find your body. How exciting!"

"I'm ecstatic," Jane muttered. "This is my proudest acting moment. The scene that'll win me that *BAFTA*."

Rory seemed rather amused at her reluctance to play a corpse and pointed towards a tent over in the distance. "Well, I guess we'd better get you over to hair and makeup. Get you all nice and bloodied-up."

Jane felt another rush of nausea. "Don't worry. I won't need that long in there. I feel like death already."

"Are you what they call a method actor, Jane?" Nesta asked.

Rory chuckled. "Oh, yeah. Jane will go to great lengths to prepare for her roles. This won't be the first time she's slept on the job. Remember the time you played a patient in that hospital drama? We had to wake you up twice."

Jane frowned at him. "Yes, thank you for that little reminder. I'll always be proud of that role." She marched off and was replaced by a nervous Victor. "Where is she?" the director asked. "I really don't think she's coming."

"She'll be here," said Rory.

There was a long pause, and Nesta decided to break the awkward silence. "So," she said, turning to Victor, who turned out to be very tall now that he was standing. His unusual height in addition to his slender body only solidified Nesta's comparison with Nosferatu. "How exactly do you make daytime look like night?"

Victor was loathed to have to answer such a basic question regarding his craft but decided to humour the woman after a long sigh. "Most of the work is done in post-production. The light has to be perfectly even when we shoot it. But it's still not ideal."

"We don't really have a choice," said Rory. "Either we shoot it in the daytime or it's not going to happen." He could tell that his comments had annoyed his director and was just about to dish out some more bad news, when he was distracted by the appearance of their lead actor. "Here she is," he said. "I told you."

Debbie Backes entered the Roman Gardens like a ruling queen after a journey through the blazing-hot desert. Her neck had returned to its normal size but her face was still puffy and red. The hair and makeup team wanted to gasp at the realisation of the impossible task they now had of making their star look like she *hadn't* just morphed into a giant lobster.

"How long is this going to take?" was the first question that Debbie had for her worried director.

"Depends on how many takes we do," his first assistant director muttered.

Debbie turned to Rory and glared. "What was that?"

"I think he meant that it shouldn't take long at all," said Victor.

The actor let out a grunt and headed off to a chair with her name on the back.

Rory stared at his director with a weary expression. Something told him that it was going to be a long morning.

CHAPTER 8

A hot and flustered Debbie Backes sat in her chair whilst fanning herself down. It felt obscene that there wasn't someone arranged to do this task for her, but that was exactly what she expected from a film of this budget. She really deserved her own trailer, she thought, and had been furious to have her request denied. It was a whole ten-minute walk from the hotel to the set, and a decent trailer would have given her the privacy that she needed.

It didn't help that there appeared to be someone sitting nearby, and the woman's presence was making her very uncomfortable. The name on the back of her deck chair said *Redman*, who Debbie assumed was her supporting actor. She was terrible with names but was pretty certain that the woman playing the dead corpse in this scene was supposed to be younger than this person.

"Shouldn't you be in hair and makeup?" Debbie asked.

Nesta turned to her and smiled. "Who, me?" She saw Debbie staring at the name on the back of her chair. "Oh, I'm not Jane Redman. She said I could sit here whilst she's getting all bloodied-up."

"Is that right?" Debbie asked. Personally, she would never have given her chair up for anyone — not even if they were on crutches. As far as she was concerned, it was her divine right to sit on that chair and had toiled away for her entire career to earn it.

"We've met before actually," said Nesta. "In the hotel room?" The other woman gave her a blank stare and shook her head. "The severed hand?"

The mere mention of the bloodied prop caused Debbie to straighten up in her chair and go an even darker shade of red. "Oh, yes, yes. Uh, of course. I thought you looked familiar." She let out a tired groan. "It's been one thing after the next on this shoot."

Nesta still couldn't contain her excitement at being sat in her very own actor's chair. She could picture herself running through her lines whilst a production assistant fetched her a coffee. Speaking of which, she thought, where was that delightful young runner? She was absolutely parched. "It must be nerve-wracking doing a big scene like this," she said, gazing at the busy crew members, as they set up their large cameras.

Debbie scoffed. "Nervous? Pah! I've been doing this job far too long to get nervous. Nerves are a bore, quite frankly. That's what my old acting tutor used to say."

"You must be very confident," said Nesta. "I'd be terrified having those cameras up in my face, knowing that it would be up on a giant screen for thousands of people to see."

The experienced actor raised her eyebrow at the word "thousands". With any hope, it would be hundreds of thousands (if not millions).

"Nonsense," she snapped. "Fear should not even come into any of it. Acting is a honed craft. You just have to trust in the process. Every actor has their own process of preparation. I have my own specific ritual that I've kept since my theatre days. It's never failed."

Nesta was hoping that Debbie would indulge her with this so-called ritual, but they were soon interrupted by a man dressed in the style of a Victorian gentleman. This was Oliver Nash, a young and up-and-coming stage actor with a handsome face and enough charm to land him the finest agents in London. Debbie hated him with a passion, as she did most of the new generation of talent. "Those self-entitled *RADA* types," she would say.

But Debbie's dislike of him did not stop Oliver Nash from prodding this tired and exhausted bear.

"Good morning, Debs." Oliver knew she hated that name, and so he used it as often as he could. "Ready for our big scene?"

Debbie glared at him. The actor was playing her onscreen accomplice — her Watson to her Holmes, except she suspected that the man fresh out of drama school probably didn't even know who Arthur Conan Doyle was. His character, Bamber, was supposed to be very intelligent. However, she had deduced that Oliver was about as bright as the empty light stand placed nearby.

"I'm always ready," said Debbie.

"Yes, of course you are." Oliver began pacing back and forth with that uncontainable energy that a lot of actors his age seemed to possess. It made him restless, like an excited puppy who couldn't wait to play.

"I feel like I'm hogging all the lines in this scene," he said, waving around his rolled-up script. "I hope you don't mind."

Debbie began grinding her teeth and refused to give him the satisfaction of seeing her irritated. "You have a lot to learn if you're still counting lines. Some of the best performances in cinema history have come from uttering a few words."

"That's good news for you, then." Oliver studied the woman's face and could feel her composure breaking.

"Acting is about what you do in the silence. Dialogue is merely a garnish."

Oliver nodded as though he understood perfectly. "I suppose you didn't even have any sound back in your day. We studied the silent era in drama school."

Nesta watched the entire exchange with a sudden level of sympathy for the older thespian. She knew what it was like to have a younger accomplice in her company (not that Debbie and Oliver were actually a team — at least away from the camera). Sometimes the lion had to give that outspoken cub a good swipe with its paw.

"Did you bring your lucky charm with you?" Oliver asked with a smirk.

Debbie cringed and pulled up the necklace hanging down from her neck. Until now, the pear-shaped diamond cradled in its centrepiece had been concealed beneath her dress and hypnotised the two people beside her. "This is not just a lucky charm," Debbie snapped, caressing the stone with her fingertips. "The Backes diamond has been in my family for generations. It was named after my great, great grandfather Gregory Backes, who discovered it whilst travelling around Europe. They say it was cut by Louis XIV before it got lost during the French Revolution."

Oliver failed to conceal his yawn. "Surprised he didn't sell it. Probably worth a few bob."

"Sell it?" Debbie asked in horror. "You simply don't sell The Backes Diamond. It's a living, breathing lifeforce. It will outlive all of us." She stared at it, lovingly. "It even saved my father's life."

The young man beside her rolled his eyes. "They're all the

rage, aren't they? Those crystals and everything. People think they have healing powers."

"I can assure you this is not one of those," Debbie snapped.

"It's beautiful," said Nesta, leaning forward to get a better look. "How did it save your father's life?"

Debbie smiled. She thought they would never ask. "He was walking at the side of the road one night in the pitch black and suffered a cardiac arrest. A passing car stopped to help him after spotting a small flashing light. Turns out he was wearing the diamond around his neck after taking it to a work event. It just caught the car headlight. Without that stranger's help, he probably would have died."

"Sounds like your old man was quite the storyteller," said Oliver.

His cynical tone infuriated his co-star, and, before she could snap at him again, Nesta decided to interrupt: "So, do you find it gives you good luck?"

Debbie turned her attention away from Oliver and sighed. "It's not about luck. It's energy." She lifted up her necklace. "I wear it at all times — even to bed. And I've worn it on every acting job I've ever done. It gives me just the right amount of power to tackle a scene. I can literally feel the energy coursing through my veins."

"I find *Red Bull* does the same for me," said Oliver with a cheeky smirk.

Debbie ignored him again and focused on Nesta. "Whenever I try to get into character, I find holding this for a minute or two always does the trick."

"Whatever works, I imagine." Nesta took one last look at the precious gemstone before it disappeared again.

Oliver had turned his attention to the park entrance and let out an excited grin. "Watch yourselves," he said. "The governor's in town."

A confused Debbie turned to see what he was looking at, and her eyes widened. "Bergman? He's *here*?!"

Nesta looked over the back of her chair to see a man with bright white hair and sunglasses over in the distance. He was wearing a sharp suit, and his teeth appeared to be whiter than his hair.

Rory came walking over to the actor's chairs with a concerned expression on his face. "Dear God," he muttered. "He's really here."

"*Who's* here?" asked Nesta. She could see that the mood on set had shifted dramatically since the appearance of this man, who reminded her of a strange cross between Andy Warhol and Don Johnson. There was no doubt in her mind that, whoever this man was, he most certainly wasn't British. Only an American could ever possess the larger-than-life aura that Jay Bergman had. It was as if a giant hand had lifted up a Hollywood businessman and planted him down directly in the overcast streets of Chester.

"Who is this man?" asked Nesta. She turned to see that Debbie had completely vanished from her chair and was now greeting the person in question with open arms.

"He's our Executive Producer," said Oliver with a disgusted shake of his head. "In other words — he's the money."

"How much money?"

"A *lot* of money." The young actor pulled a packet of chewing gum from his pocket and began munching away.

Nesta found it strange to see someone dressed like a Victorian gentleman chewing at the rate of a modern day football manager. "He sounds like a big deal," she said.

"Sure is," said Oliver. "No Jay, no movie. Rumour has it, he saved this production when a load of our financiers dropped out. But everything comes at a cost." He looked over at his nervous director, crouching down against an ancient stone.

"Victor will tell you all about that. These American producers are all sharks. Half of them make their money in other industries and act like they're creative geniuses. Jay apparently told Victor that he made all his fortunes in zinc. But he's liked movies since he was a child and enjoys being involved. *Too* involved if you ask me." He let out a *huff*. "But nobody asks me, obviously."

"Surely a businessman like him would leave you professionals to it," said Nesta, watching the various crew members rush over to make a fuss of the man.

Oliver chuckled. "Yeah, right. If there's one thing I've learnt in the film industry so far it's this — everyone thinks they can make their own movie. This Jay guy's been sticking his nose in every department. Including the casting. And there's nothing anyone can do about it. It's his money."

Nesta nodded. That explained Debbie's sudden enthusiasm, she thought. "It all sounds very cut-throat."

"You have no idea," said Oliver. His chewing slowed. "That man is as cold-blooded as they come. He'd axe his own mother if he didn't like how she was performing."

They both watched the producer howling with laughter. His black sunglasses and ultra-white teeth made him resemble a certain great white predator even more, and Nesta couldn't help but shudder.

CHAPTER 9

Victor peered through his viewfinder to get another look at the shot. Everything was in place, but he still wasn't happy with the framing. No matter how many times his camera operator changed the angle, the wide shot just didn't match what he had seen in his head. The frustrated director took a step back to get a better look of the set.

Jane Redman was in the same position that she would be for the entire scene, lying in the grass with a layer of artificial blood across her face. It was far from comfortable, and she much preferred her time on *Holby City*, where there was a nice, comfy hospital bed with a thick pillow.

Debbie and Oliver were standing in the middle of the frame, as a smoke machine kept blowing out large clouds over them. Both actors were forced to face each other whilst their director made his finishing touches.

"At least it's not that horrible artificial snow," Oliver muttered with gritted teeth. It was the longest that he and Debbie had looked into each other's eyes, and he felt her glaring into his soul with that piercing stare.

Debbie was nowhere near as optimistic. "We should really have stand-ins for this kind of thing. Why aren't we rolling yet?"

Oliver smiled. "You can't rush art."

Their first assistant director, Rory, would beg to differ. He glanced at his watch for the umpteenth time and marched over to Victor. "We really need to get this done."

"The shot looks rubbish," Victor snapped.

Rory took a look at the nearby monitor and squinted. "Looks alright to me."

"Alright?! I've been planning this scene for months. You want me to just point the camera and shoot like some third-rate television programme?"

His assistant director shrugged. "If we don't shoot something, then there won't be any film at all. Besides, it's just the wide shot. Most of the scene will be close-ups anyway."

Victor glared at him. "You want to direct this film instead now?"

Rory squared up to him and puffed out his chest. "Maybe I should! At least we'll all get lunch that way."

The two men were interrupted by Jay Bergman, who caused them both to back off each other. "Everything alright, gentleman?" the producer asked in his Californian accent.

"Absolutely," said Rory with a forced smile. He put his arm around the director. "Victor here was just telling me how great the wide shot is looking."

Jay checked his watch. "Shouldn't we have this scene in the can already?"

"Yes!" Rory clapped his hands. "That's a great idea. We were just about to start rolling."

Moments later, and the cameras were fired up and ready to go.

Nesta stood on the sidelines, bursting with anticipation. She couldn't wait to catch her first glimpse of *The Shilling Murders*, and it was like she had her own exclusive preview. Maybe they needed a few more extras, she thought, and pictured herself immortalised on screen. She could surprise Darren and tell him that she was now a film star (not that he would ever watch anything that didn't have explosions and a car chase).

As her mind began plotting out a way to make her little goal come true, she spotted a certain Hollywood producer standing beside the tea cart.

"I've got a good feeling about this film," she said. "I think it's going to be a blockbuster."

Jay Bergman scoffed. "This movie's been a circus since the very beginning. It'll be a miracle if it breaks even at this rate. I knew we should've used a studio."

"Surely you can't beat filming in a wonderful city like Chester?" Nesta asked.

The producer slipped down his sunglasses to take a better look at the woman standing beside him. The flash of daylight almost blinded him, and he pushed them back up like a suffering vampire. "Are you for real? We got people back in LA who can make anything. And we'd do a better job than the Romans did. I shot a whole period drama two years ago in a Burbank sound stage. It's cheaper and easier." He looked up to see a black cloud approaching. "We also don't have to be worried about the weather."

"If you don't mind me asking," said Nesta. "Why exactly did you want to produce a British film in the first place?"

Jay laughed and exposed those expensive teeth. "You got me there. Worst decision I ever made." He ran a hand through his white hair. "But what can I say — I'm a sentimental type. I loved the book, and the author insisted it had to be filmed in the UK or we wouldn't get the rights. Plus, I thought it would be a chance to get back to my roots. I got a soft spot for this island. My family all hail from across the border."

Nesta's face lit up. "You have Welsh blood?"

The producer nodded. "You betcha!" He rolled up his sleeve to reveal a Welsh dragon tattooed on his forearm. "My mother's side of the family tree are all from this town called Builth Wells."

"I know Builth very well," said Nesta. "I'm from Bala, myself."

"No kidding!" Jay lowered his glasses again. "You're Welsh? I thought that accent of yours wasn't English. How about that? We're practically family."

"Iechyd da!"

The producer stared at her. "Come again?"

"It's Welsh for cheers. Iechyd da!"

Jay laughed. "Yeah? I like that! Iekkie Da!" He turned to a nearby sound engineer, who seemed to be in his own world. "You hear that, sound guy? I'm talking Welsh! Ieggy Do!" He clapped his hands and cackled. "So, what's your role on this movie, sweetheart?"

Nesta felt a surge of panic. She had enjoyed her little morning on the film set and couldn't bear the idea of being kicked out just yet. "Oh," she said. "I do a bit of everything, you see." A sly grin crept across her face. "Although, what I'd really like to get into is background work."

"Background?" asked Jay.

"That's what they call it, isn't it? Background artist? The people who move about in the background?"

The producer smirked. "You mean, a movie extra? Ha-ha! Background artist — is that what they call it around here? I guess sitting around pretending to talk could be considered an artform — maybe to crazy people."

"I heard one of the crew members mention it earlier," said Nesta. "I think they prefer a more official title these days."

Jay rolled his eyes. "Whatever floats their boat." He turned to the Welsh woman with a sentimental look on his face that really didn't suit him. "You really want to be an extra in this thing?"

"More than anything," said Nesta. She clasped her hands and gazed up towards the sky as though she were a child making a wish.

"Well, you know what?" The producer clicked his fingers and winked. "I think we can make that happen."

"You really think so?"

"I know so!" The man straightened up his tie and jiggled his head. "This is my movie. And I can do whatever I want. I'm sure we can find you a scene. Maybe even a line."

"Oh, heavens! Come, now, Mr Bergman. You would do that for me?" Nesta wouldn't normally trust this producer as far as she could throw him. She knew a shrewd businessman when she saw one, and Jay Bergman was as sharp as they came. But, if he allowed her to make a tiny appearance in this highly-antici-pated film, she was more than happy to feed his ego. Anything so that she could get to try on a Victorian costume and wander around like someone from a Charles Dickens novel. Her late husband would have found the whole thing hysterical, and she couldn't wait to tell her daughter (who seemed to think that her mother was incapable of doing anything remotely interesting).

"As far as I'm concerned," said Jay, placing his hand on her shoulder. "You and I are practically family. And families need to take care of each other."

"Well," said Nesta. "That's very thoughtful of you." She was struck by a sudden breeze and really wanted to tell him not to wear so much aftershave (but there was no point jeopardising her new film career now).

"Everybody stand by!" Rory cried out, as his crew began running to their positions. "We're about to go for a take!"

"Finally," Jay muttered under his breath.

Nesta watched Debbie Backes pull out her trusty necklace to

give it a quick stroke. The actor was already transcending into her character and was ready to break a leg.

"She's such a talented actor, don't you think?"

Nesta's question caused the producer to turn and frown. "Who? Debbie Backes?" The man let out a grunt. "The woman's a liability. I never wanted her in the first place. Nobody in the States even knows who the hell she is."

"You've never seen *Steeping Road*?" asked Nesta.

"A dumb soap opera?" asked Jay. "I'd rather watch my car go rusty." His usual public-facing smile had vanished and his expression turned sour at the sight of his lead actor preparing for a take. "I had the perfect actor for the role. A real star of the big screen. But Debbie was already attached to the project when I came on board. Unfortunately, this other production company we have is putting in thirty percent of the money, and Debbie was part of the deal. I was hoping to change their mind once we headed into pre-production, but they wouldn't budge."

"Is this other production company British?"

"Yep. And they don't seem to have a clue what they're doing. Bunch of amateurs. The company's owner assured me they would take care of the production side, and I could just sit back and relax. But you know what they say — if you need a job doing properly..." His gaze landed on a man standing on the other side of the gardens. "There he is right now. Our beloved British producer."

Nesta looked across the set to see the producer he was referring to — a restless and seemingly anxious Felix Melvin, who was busy pacing back and forth on his mobile phone. Suddenly, the controversy of Debbie Backes' casting became clear, and she wondered whether the American knew that Felix was also Debbie's nephew.

"Quiet please!" Rory was standing beside the two actors taking centre stage and raised up his arms to get everyone's attention. "Everyone standing by!" He looked over at his director for the signal. Victor was sat behind his monitors and gave him the thumbs up.

"Roll sound!" Victor called out.

"Sound rolling!"

"Roll cameras!"

"Cameras rolling!"

The entire set went silent, and the crew were hanging on the first assistant director's every word.

"Action!"

Debbie stood in a cloud of artificial mist and glared down over the body of Jane Redman. She allowed for a long, dramatic pause before delivering her first line: "I think we were too late, Bamber."

A serious Oliver nodded beside her and lowered an old pipe from his mouth. "Yes, Ma'm. I think we are."

There was another long pause, and Debbie knelt down to inspect the body. "I recognise this woman. She works as a secretary down at —" The actor began to stutter, and she closed her eyes in despair.

"*Booth and Sons*!" Victor cried out. "It's *Booth and Sons*!"

"Cut!" Rory cried, and the crew began running around. "Everyone reset!"

"I knew it was *Booth and Sons*!" Debbie roared. "You silly man! I was pausing for effect. Don't you know proper acting when you see it? Now you've ruined a perfectly good take!"

The furious director tried to restrain himself from shouting out something that he would later regret, and it wasn't long before everyone was back in their starting positions again.

"Ready — *action*!"

The Roman Gardens went silent, and Nesta watched with great fascination. She was so used to watching films from the comfort of her front living room that she had forgotten about the reality of how they were made. She was aware that each scene needed to be repeated multiple times and from various different angles, but it was still strange to witness the process in person. The performances were far more subtle than a stage play, and the whole thing felt rather underwhelming. She hoped that, with a touch of editing and music, her favourite scene would translate a lot better on the screen.

The cameras were rolling again, and Debbie's bottom lip began to quiver. Beads of sweat began forming along her forehead, and she felt her heart race.

"I think we were too late, Bamber."

"Yes, Ma'm. I think we are."

Debbie knelt down and heard a loud cry.

"Argh!!" Jane cried out. The dead corpse had seemingly come to life and was clutching her thigh in pain. "That was my leg you just put all your weight on!"

"Don't talk rubbish!" Debbie snapped. "I never miss my marks! Your leg was in the wrong place..."

"Cut!" Rory cried out. "Let's reset as quickly as we can!"

Jay Bergman had begun burying his distraught face in the palm of his hand, as Debbie continued berating her co-star.

"What sort of actor are you?" she asked. "The last time I checked, dead bodies were supposed to remain still!"

"Going again!" Rory cried. "*Action!*"

Debbie's face was now resembling that of the dead corpse, and she tried to remain calm.

"I think we were too late, Bamber."

"Yes, Ma'm. I think we are."

This time, she managed to kneel down against her mark, and Jane's leg was spared.

"This person looks familiar, Bamber. I've seen her before. I, uh, I'm certain of it. Why, she — she —"

"*Cut!!*" Victor screamed, much to the surprise of his assistant director, who considered that to be his responsibility. "Cut, cut, cut!" He lifted up the script and waved it at his lead actor. "That's not even the right line!"

"It's called improvisation!" Debbie cried back.

"We're adapting a piece of literature!" Victor snapped. "There's no room for improvisation!"

Debbie scoffed. "Literature? Pah!" She stormed across the set and grabbed a spare copy of the paperback. "You call this toilet-reading piece of formulaic rubbish *literature*?"

The argument continued for another ten minutes, and Nesta turned to the distraught American producer still standing beside her. "Now, I don't know much about filmmaking, but would you say that it's going well, so far?"

Jay Bergman couldn't even bring himself to answer her question and walked off in search of his drink flask.

CHAPTER 10

Nesta arrived back at *The Legion Hotel* a lot later than she had expected. Unsurprisingly, the filming over at the Roman Gardens had carried on well into the afternoon and didn't finish until the sun began to dip behind the Chester rooftops.

When Nesta approached the hotel entrance, the doorman, Malcolm, was in his usual spot outside, whilst the younger porter struggled with a trolley full of bags.

"That's it, Henry. Show that trolley who's boss."

Henry took his attention off the luggage for a moment to give his colleague a harsh frown. "Why can't I be the one standing by the door?"

Malcolm sighed. "You don't simply become a doorman overnight. We all have to earn our stripes. When I was your age, we didn't even have a trolley. Your time will come, lad. Being a doorman is whole different skillet."

"Looks pretty easy to me," Henry muttered, silently enough so that the man couldn't hear him. He braced himself for another push and managed to knock the largest suitcase completely off the trolley.

"Will you be careful with that?" asked the disgruntled owner of this stray piece of luggage. "That bag is worth more than you are!"

Malcolm watched his colleague scramble around to retrieve the case and shook his head. "Dear, dear. Poor boy. It seems you still have so much to learn." The doorman turned to see Nesta approaching the door and tipped his hat. "Good evening, madam! Are you enjoying your stay so far?"

Nesta gave him a suspicious nod. She suspected that the man was merely doing his job and didn't believe for one second that he really cared about her stay.

"Is he alright?" she asked, pointing at the struggling young porter, who was busy trying to reposition the fallen suitcase like a giant game of *Jenga*.

"He'll get there," said Malcolm. "You know what these young people are like. No common sense."

Nesta knew all about young people and could agree that they could be a little hard work at times. "I wouldn't be too hard on him. He seems to be trying his best."

Malcolm chuckled. "Don't be fooled. You give him an inch, and he'll take a mile. I often catch him hiding in the storeroom, playing on that phone of his. He's sneakier than he looks."

"Don't get me started on phones," said Nesta with a groan. "I know a teenager who's practically connected to one."

The doorman nodded. "They'll be the death of this next generation." He watched the young porter wheel away the trolley whilst a concerned guest followed closely behind. "Don't tell him I said this, but he's a good egg really. The lad's been through quite a lot. He's my nephew, you see."

"I thought there was a slight resemblance." Nesta was starting to see a new side to the man who had questioned her arrival on the very first day. She had initially taken a disliking to his strict nature and stubborn adherence to the rules (despite her having a similar reputation as a teacher), but, for a split second, Nesta had spotted a warmth behind that formal facade.

"Henry's mother passed away when he was just a boy," said Malcolm with a sadness in his eyes. "She was my little sister, God bless her. So, I took Henry to live with me. I treat him like a son, but he still prefers to call me Uncle Malcolm. There was a very large age gap between me and Chloe. She was more like a daughter at times. It's funny, considering that I've never had children of my own."

Nesta could sense the man's discomfort. She couldn't imagine that he normally shared something this personal with a passing guest and was taken aback by his openness with her. "I'm sorry to hear about your sister." Malcolm gave her an appreciative nod. "What about Henry's father?"

The man coughed into his gloved hand. "He turned out to be a — well, I won't use the word I would choose to describe what *he* was. But when my sister got terminally ill, he decided to leave and never come back."

"I can think of a few words to describe what he was," said Nesta with a look of disgust.

Malcolm smiled and nodded. "Yes, he really showed his true colours in the end, that man."

"And so did you. Taking in your nephew like that."

Malcolm looked up to see the admiration in her face. It had taken him by surprise and caused a short silence in their conversation.

"Oh," he said, eventually. "It's what anyone in my position would have done." He checked to make sure that the porter was safely out of earshot. "Again, never tell him this, but Henry's the best thing that ever happened to me."

Nesta gave him a warm smile. "I think that's something he should hear. You should probably tell him one day."

The doorman blushed and removed his hat for a moment to

scratch his head. He tried to remind himself of his duty and stood tall like a trained soldier. "Anyway," he said with an embarrassed cough. "You don't need to hear anymore of my gibberish. You're supposed to be on holiday." The man tipped his hat. "Have a lovely evening, madam."

Nesta approached the doors and smiled back at him. "Call me Nesta."

THE BUBBLE BATH idea had been a splendid one. When at home, Nesta opted for the usual quick shower as her method for getting clean. But she wasn't at home now, and the opportunity to fulfill her late husband's passion for trying out complimentary soaps had been too much to resist.

Lying back in a cloud of soapy foam, Nesta let out a long, deep breath. *This* was a holiday, she thought. Her recent caravanning experience on the Flintshire coast had failed to satisfy her craving for a little bit of luxury and indulgence. A few days at the beach just hadn't quite cut the mustard, especially when most of the sand seemed to find its way home with her.

That evening, there was not a sand granule in sight, and she was looking forward to another night in her very own king-sized bed.

Her entire body was the most relaxed it had been in quite some time, and she could feel her mind drifting off into a meditative state. Just as she was about to close her eyes, Nesta heard a voice call out from the other side of the bathroom wall. Her body went tense, as her moment of zen was shattered by a chilling scream.

CHAPTER 11

The scream had come from the room next door. Nesta had leapt out of the bath as though someone had filled it with an entire bucket of ice. She grabbed the nearest towel, wrapped herself up, and went running out into the hallway. Unlike the last time there had been a disturbing noise coming from Debbie Backes' room, the entire hallway was empty.

Holding her towel tight, Nesta made a dash for Room Thirty-Five and was surprised to find that the door was wide open. She entered the room with her jaw fully lowered. Debbie Backes was lying at the side of the bed with a steak knife lodged straight into her chest. Her dressing gown was no longer white, and a member of the hotel staff was sobbing beside her.

"She's dead!" the young woman cried. "She's dead!"

Nesta rushed over to comfort her and took a quick scan of the room. She could hear the shower still running over in the bathroom, and there was a plate of half-eaten steak on the edge of the bed. Everything else looked similar to how she had seen it on her first day. Either way, it was clear that the person responsible for Debbie Backes' death was long gone.

THE YOUNG WOMAN'S name was Amy. She usually spent the majority of her shift in the hotel dining room, serving guests their food. After the horrors of her discovery in Debbie Backes' room, she had not left Nesta's side for the rest of the evening. The police had been quick to arrive, and the first people they needed to question were their only two witnesses (as far as Nesta knew).

Nesta and Amy spent the majority of their time sitting in the hotel lobby, whilst the police did their job of turning a single hotel room into a full-scale crime scene. Naturally, the entire discovery had caused quite a stir, and hotel manager Elliott was beside himself with stress.

"Can I get you two anything else?" he asked, pacing around the lobby like a father in a maternity ward. "Something to eat? Something to drink?"

"I think we're fine," said Nesta. Her arm was back around Amy's shoulders, who had erupted into another bout of sobbing. "It's alright," she said. "You're still in shock. It'll all be over soon."

Nesta watched the various members of the crime scene investigation team darting back and forth like busy bees. The detective on the case was busy interviewing another person on the other side of the lobby, and she made a mental note to remember the face. Nesta was certain that she had seen this woman on the film set, holding up that strange, fluffy object on the end of a pole. Why the police had chosen to question *this* person, she would have to find out later.

"What happens now?" Amy asked, drying her eyes.

"The police will want to question everyone they can," said Nesta. "And they'll be going over that hotel room with a fine tooth comb before removing the body." Her use of the last word sent Amy straight back into a sob.

"I thought she'd taken a fall when I first walked in," Amy said. "It wouldn't be the first time that happened in this hotel. We once had a guest who collapsed in his room from too much alcohol. And another who fainted. We thought *that* person was dead at first, but he turned out to be diabetic."

"I think we can be pretty certain that this guest isn't getting up again," said Nesta, visualising that knife lodged in Debbie's chest. "What brought you to her room in the first place?"

Amy tried to keep herself together. "Mrs Backes likes a gin and tonic brought to her room. She'd ordered one specially, about half an hour before I came up."

"Why did it take so long?" Nesta asked.

"Debbie had specifically asked to have it delivered in thirty minutes," said Amy. "She was planning to have it after her shower. Debbie's like clockwork. Every day at six o'clock she has a snack before taking her shower. Then she has her gin and tonic."

"She calls a fillet steak a snack?" Nesta was more partial to some cheddar and crackers, but, then again, *her* meals weren't going down on a film production's expenses. She shook her head and thought about Debbie's call for room service, which implied that there would have been a thirty-minute window for the killer to enter the room and leave again (a very generous window at that). *How* and *why* the killer did this were far more difficult questions to answer. Nesta had only been given one room key, and she presumed that Debbie had the same. The door did not appear to be broken, and so a forced entry was out of the question. If there was indeed a second key, then whoever had it still in their possession was at the top of the suspect list. The third (and most unlikely) option was that Debbie had let her killer into the room, making him or her as cold-blooded as they come. To be murdered by someone a person knew (however common) was surely the cruelest fate anyone could imagine. If you couldn't trust a friend or a family member, then who could you trust?

Nesta sat in silence for a while, her mind whirling away, as she worked through all of the possible scenarios (and there were many of them). This was not the first murder she had come across, but it was certainly the most high profile. She had witnessed many soap stars killed on screen, including some elaborate deaths that often tested the realms of plausibility. Like her character, Appie, Debbie Backes had finally met her maker, only this time, everything hadn't paused for a dramatic cliffhanger. In real life, there were no theme song or credit sequence — just the harsh consequences of a brutal action.

"Who on earth would *do* something like that?" Amy asked her.

Nesta could not give the young woman a definitive answer, but she was certainly determined to find out. As soon as she got the chance, Nesta would be making a call to someone else who might be interested in such a mystery, a person who, thanks to the school summer holidays, had a lot of time on his hands.

CHAPTER 12

Nesta's text message had come at just the right time. It may have read like a handwritten letter (there was not a single abbreviation or acronym and no emojis in sight), but the communication had been clear enough. Darren Price had spent the best part of his week trying to complete the latest *Fortnite* game and was pleased to have succeeded in record time. Therefore, the rest of his summer holidays looked rather bleak, and he was destined to kill his time loitering the high street of Bala.

His online streaming channel (now devoted entirely to true crime) had gone from strength to strength since the coverage of Mold's unlikely shooting outside of St Mary's Church. He had even amassed a new legion of American followers, who found the adventures of a retired teacher and his teenage assistant quite delightful. In Darren's mind, views were views, and he would have quite happily filmed himself jumping off a rooftop if it had meant new followers. And, so, a brand new murder was quite welcome. Despite Nesta's lengthy text message, he was still short on the details of this latest crime, but he *had* been promised a few nights of accommodation in a swanky Chester hotel (and he couldn't refuse that). The only part of the offer that made him slightly apprehensive was the fact that he had been asked to bring along a sleeping bag. Surely, there would be complimentary sheets and a duvet, he thought to himself, but the teenager had never stayed in a hotel before and didn't want to take any chances.

Incredibly, it had taken no further buses for him to reach Chester's bustling Pepper Street as it had done to get to Mold high street (with only a short changeover at Wrexham bus station). After a short walk to Love Street, Darren was faced with the grand exterior of *The Legion Hotel*.

"Nice," he muttered to himself, as he looked up at the building's impressive entrance. The teenager headed over to the main doors and began messaging his contact.

"Sorry, young man," said a male voice behind him. "There'll be no loitering out here."

Darren looked up to see a stern doorman.

Malcolm was gazing down at the teenager's tattered trainers and ripped jeans. They had been enough to make his mind up about this suspicious young fellow. "Come on," he said. "Move along."

"Chillout, *Beverly Hills Cop*." Darren ignored the man's frown and returned to his screen. "I'm a guest at this hotel." He swung the rucksack off from his shoulder. "Actually, you can take my bag, if you like?"

Malcolm's face turned a bright shade of red, and he prepared to give the teenager a right earful.

"It's alright, Malcom." Nesta was now standing behind them with a warm smile. "He's with me."

The doorman restrained himself from unleashing the tirade of abuse and turned to Nesta with a smile. "Sorry, Nesta. I hadn't realised."

Nesta saw the suspicion in the man's face and decided to think on her feet. "He's my grandson."

Darren raised an eyebrow.

"Well," said Malcolm with a satisfied nod. "That explains it. Come along, then, lad. Don't keep your grandmother waiting." He signalled for him to join her, and Nesta gave an appreciative nod.

The teenager reluctantly obliged and, once they were safely through the main doors, turned to Nesta with a frown. "Please, don't ever call me that in public again."

They continued past the reception desk, and Nesta gave Frida a friendly wave.

"Wow," said Darren. "You seem to have made yourself at home."

After a short elevator trip and a stroll along the fourth floor, Nesta escorted her guest inside his new room. "The police have cordoned off most of the third floor," she said, when they entered. "So, I've been given a new room. Although, it looks practically identical to the last one."

An impressed Darren did a quick scan of her new sleeping quarters and asked a more important question: "So which floor's *my* room on?"

Nesta gave him a blank stare. "This *is* your room." She received a blank stare in return.

"I thought you said this was *your* room," said Darren.

They both stared at each other until the teenager finally caught on. "Oh, please, no..." He took another look at the king-sized bed. "You want me to share a room with you?!"

His new roommate rolled her eyes and sighed. "Why else did you think I asked you to bring a sleeping bag?"

Darren began pacing around the room, as the reality of his situation started to sink in. "I thought I'd at least have my own hotel room!"

"Do you know how much a room here costs?" asked Nesta. "Don't you dare touch anything in there!" The teenager paused his inspection of the minibar and groaned. "I might as well be homeless!"

"Don't be daft." Nesta chucked one of her pillows on the small sofa beside the window. "At least you won't be on the floor. Besides, it's not like you've got much choice now that you're here. You won't find anywhere else in this city at such a late hour."

A sulking Darren plonked himself down on the sofa. "This is entrapment."

Nesta shook her head. "I don't think entrapment means what you think it means."

"If it means forcing someone to sleep rough for the night, then it means *exactly* what I think it means."

"You know there's breakfast included?"

The young man's ears pricked up. "There is? Like *actual* breakfast — not some other play on words?"

"Did you want to be involved in this thing or not?" Nesta asked. "Or does Bala have another murder you could be looking into?"

Darren folded up his arms and huffed. "Alright, why don't you start by filling me in on this Debbie woman."

Nesta took a deep breath. She realised that this was going to take a lot longer than she thought. "You've really never seen the television soap *Steeping Road*?"

"My mam used to watch," said Darren. "It always looked rubbish."

"Sounds like you really *haven't* seen it," said Nesta, grinding her teeth. "The woman murdered in her hotel room was one of *Steeping Road*'s biggest stars. She's been in it since the beginning."

"Then why is she in a film?"

"This was supposed to be her big break into movies."

"Isn't she a little old to be looking for big breaks?"

Darren's question evoked a fierce stare from Nesta. He had said something very dangerous, and the teenager was already regretting it.

"It's never too late to try something new," Nesta snapped. "You'll learn that someday. People spend their whole lives talking about doing something different. Before you know it, forty years have gone by, and they're still doing the same thing. You'll do well to remember that."

"Alright, alright." Darren held up his imaginary white flag. "What I *meant* was — acting is acting. Why didn't she just keep doing the soap thing?"

Nesta sighed. "I suppose some people consider soaps to be a lesser art form. Personally, I would have preferred if she stayed on *Steeping Road*." She was struck by a sudden, chilling thought. There would have been a few *Steeping Road* fans upset at the departure of a series regular like Debbie Backes. She may have not been cross enough herself to commit such an act of violence over the matter but wouldn't have put it past some people. "I wonder if Debbie's departure has been made public yet..."

"Hmh?" asked Darren.

"Oh, it's nothing. I just know that some fans can be quite passionate about their heroes." Nesta turned to see that the teenager was now spread out across her bed. "At least take your shoes off first!"

Darren jumped and almost rolled off onto the floor. "You think some crazy fan did it?" he asked.

Nesta shook her head. "Who knows. There are plenty of other suspects to consider first."

"Like — who?"

"Well, Debbie could be something of a diva when she wanted to be."

"Ah," said Darren with a nod. "You're thinking the hotel staff.

Gotcha." Suddenly he became a little worried. He wasn't overly keen on the idea of staying the night in a hotel where the staff had a history of murdering their guests. "Have you been making sure to tip them, by the way?"

Nesta rolled her eyes. "I was more concerned about her production crew. Most of them are staying at the hotel." She pulled a disgusted face. "Then there's that whole business with the severed hand on the pillow."

Darren's eyes widened, and, this time, he leapt off the bed completely. "What kind of creepy hotel is this?"

"I'll tell you all about that later," said Nesta, who couldn't help but be amused by the teenager's sudden paranoia. Served him right for not taking his shoes off, she thought. "There have been a couple of pranks over the last few days. Someone really had it in for that woman. But enough to kill her with a steak knife? I can't say."

"Steak knife?" asked Darren. "What makes you think it was for cutting steak?"

Nesta placed both hands firmly on her hips. "Believe it or not, but I do know my way around a kitchen. My cooking isn't that bad."

"Is it better than your baking?" Darren flinched, as Nesta reminded him of a rhino about to charge.

"If you're not careful, Darren Price, you'll be sleeping on the streets of Chester tonight."

There was that old, familiar teacher's voice, Darren thought (but very wisely decided to keep the observation to himself).

"So we could be looking at a killer chef?" he asked.

Nesta took her rightful place on the king-sized bed and sat herself down, whilst her guest made do with the sofa. "I wouldn't be surprised given the peanut mash incident." She smiled at her own inappropriate joke and saw the confusion in Darren's face. "Oh, yes. I'll need to fill you in on that whole thing, too." She heard her stomach begin to rumble. "Speaking of which, would you care to join me for dinner later? The hotel has a wonderful dining room. And I get a fifty-percent discount."

Darren stared at her in disbelief. She hadn't exactly sold it to him. The prospect of having his food prepared by a murdering member of the kitchen staff was hardly appetising. But, then again, he never turned down a free meal.

CHAPTER 13

Darren had never worn a shirt to dinner in his entire life, and he wasn't about to start that night. Shirts were strictly for funerals and weddings only (not that he had been to many of those), and when he entered *The Legion Hotel* dining hall in a vintage *Iron Maiden* t-shirt, he certainly turned a few heads.

Fortunately for him, many of the guests were members of the film crew and had a tendency to dress down themselves.

Nesta had opted for a more casual attire herself this time around and was surprised to find a full house when they arrived. It appeared that Debbie's death had not affected the crew's appetite, and many of them were even enjoying a round of drinks.

"You wouldn't know that someone has just died," said Darren, as they were escorted to their table.

"I suppose the show must go on," said Nesta.

Not everyone was in a jovial mood, however, and she noticed the film's gloomy director alone in the corner with his own bottle of wine.

"Nice t-shirt," said a passing member of the sound department, pointing to Darren's top and giving him a thumbs-up. The bearded man was dressed in a *Twisted Sister* shirt, and the teenager approved greatly.

"These people are cool," Darren said, once they were seated. "Maybe I should get a job in the film industry."

"Not until you've finished your exams," said Nesta, lifting up her menu.

"Alright, Nan." He saw her surprised reaction and raised out his arms in defence. "What? I'm practically in the media business already, anyway. The channel, remember?"

Nesta rolled her eyes. How could she forget? Darren's online true crime channel was going from strength to strength since her involvement. The teenager had kept his word about sharing the income made from their growing followers, and she had even managed to buy a new microwave.

"I think there's a big difference between internet videos and the silver screen," she said. "These people aren't making videos in their bedroom."

"We have more in common than you think," said Darren with a smug grin. "Online content is the future. These people need someone like me. I should probably do some networking. Maybe I can get a couple of days work."

"You'll have to get in line," said Nesta with an excited grin. She had been bursting to deliver her news all afternoon.

"How do you mean?" asked Darren.

"I'm going to be in the film."

The teenager raised a cynical eyebrow. "Doing *what*?"

"What do you think?" Nesta lifted up an imaginary skull like her favourite Shakespearean character. "Acting!"

Darren was even less convinced than before. "Yeah, right. What role are you playing?"

"They haven't told me yet. But I seem to remember that the

book has some dinner party scenes in a large country house. So maybe I can be a lady of high society. Like a duchess!"

"Sounds pretty boring to me. Shame it's not a gangster film."

"Well," said Nesta. "It's set in Victorian times. Maybe they can find you a role as a little pickpocket. I could imagine that."

Darren's frown caused her to laugh, and they were joined by Jane Redman.

"Evening," she said with a grin. The actor appeared to be in a very good mood.

"Hey," said Nesta. "You better watch yourself. You're not the only actor hustling for a role." She pointed at her own head. "Mr Bergman said I could be an extra. Shame there won't be a film anymore."

"Who says there's no film?" Jane's smile kept growing.

"Surely you'll be shutting down now. You've lost your lead actor?"

Jane folded up her arms and sighed. "If there's one thing I've learnt in this industry — everyone's replaceable."

Nesta was dumbfounded by the actor's confidence. "Even Debbie Backes? She's the main protagonist. How on earth would you carry on without her?"

"According to the rumours," said Jane, "they've found a way. Filmmakers have plenty of tricks up their sleeve for a scenario like this. There have been plenty of films where an actor has died half way through: Brandon Lee, Oliver Reed, Bela Lugosi..."

"But I doubt any of these were *murdered*," Nesta snapped. "Isn't it a little disrespectful?"

Jane shrugged. "There's a lot of money at stake. And money talks in this business."

Nesta shook her head and excused herself.

"Hey!" Darren called out. "Where are you going?" He watched her head off in the direction of the film director's table and returned to his overwhelming menu. "I need a translator to pick my food."

"I would avoid the mash," said Jane before walking away.

Darren frowned and quickly lost his appetite.

Victor was enjoying a quiet moment to himself, when a determined woman joined him at the table.

"Do you always sit on your own?" Nesta asked.

The director looked around the room at his fellow cast and crew members. "I like to create a little bubble for myself during a shoot. I find it helps to keep in the zone."

"I'm sure some of your crew would appreciate it if you joined them every once in a while. It would help their morale."

Victor shook his head. "They don't want me in their faces outside the set. Being a director's a lonely job. Maybe that's why I'm so good at it. You're catered for your every need, and you're mainly talking to actors. And we all know *they* don't really give a toss as long as they look good."

Nesta could see that the man was already at the bottom of his wine bottle. "Is it true that you're carrying on with the shoot?"

"Looks like it," said Victor. "The producers want to push ahead. There's too much invested to pull the plug." He stared down at the pile of storyboards scattered across the table and began pouring red wine over them. "So much for trying to make the best film we can. I should have just been a cartoonist."

"You can certainly draw," said Nesta, cringing at the stains across his papers.

"I started out as an animator." Victor let out a rare smile. It was so unusual for him that it was slightly disturbing. "Animation suited me down to the ground. It's a pure artform. You don't need sets, costumes, locations... in fact, you barely need actors! Just me and my imagination. Full creative control."

Nesta stared at one of the few storyboards that *wasn't*

covered in wine and honed in on one frame in particular. It was an image of the two main characters standing over a body. Despite the inclusion of a dead corpse, it had a certain elegance and beauty that hypnotised her for a moment. "If you don't mind me asking," she said, looking up at the miserable director, "why exactly did you become a filmmaker in the first place?"

Victor chuckled. "That's a good question. The animation studio I used to work at closed down. We specialised in hand-drawn animation, but all of our competitors had moved to solely focus on computer generated imagery. Most animations these days are CGI, even children's cartoons, and the head of our computer was too stubborn to evolve." Victor smiled again. "I liked him for that. Bob Leyland. He was one of those old school animators. Bob even worked for *Disney*, apparently. He was my mentor and hero. It was so hard to see that studio of his close. I remember, during our last meeting before I got made redundant, he told me to always follow my artistic gut. Never compromise for anyone — not for fame, management and especially not for money. He said it was a road to an empty soul. Something I'd regret for the rest of my life." He swallowed an enormous gulp of wine. "And he was right."

Nesta listened with sheer curiosity. She had never been the most creative person (unlike her sister, Mari), but she *had* dabbled with a paint brush on more than one occasion and was keen to start up her old hobby again at some point. She loved the thought of filling up a blank canvas with her water colours, letting her imagination run wild in the moment (whilst also trying to create something that at least slightly resembled a landscape). But she could never imagine some businessman marching over and telling her what to paint. There would be no fun in that at all. "So what happened after you lost your job?" she asked.

"I tried to find another one," said Victor. "I approached every animation house in London. But, unsurprisingly, all the jobs going were computer based. I didn't know the first thing about creating 3D images. I'd only ever done traditional animation. That's what I'd specialised in at art college. So, I managed to land a job making the teas and coffees on a film set. It was just something to pay the bills. The films this production company made were awful. They were mostly cheap, British gangster films using old soap actors — the kind that went straight to DVD. One afternoon, I was doodling on a break, and the producer walked past and saw my drawings. He asked me if I could do storyboards, and then said that I had a real vision. Producers are good like that for making you feel special. After a couple of months of doing storyboards, he told me that he wanted to move away from churning out exploitation flicks and produce films of a higher standard. I think he had dreams of winning awards and being taken seriously in the film industry. He said he needed a director with a highly creative mind and a clear vision. Most of the ones he had used so far were hacks from the television industry who were used to churning out episodes like a factory. So I agreed to direct his next film."

"What was the film?" asked Nesta.

Victor smiled. "An adaptation of a popular crime novel. This producer had got lucky and nabbed the film rights. It was his big chance not to blow it." He turned her attention to the two men sitting at a table on the other side of the room.

Nesta suddenly caught on. "You mean — *this* film? Felix? Felix was this producer you were talking about?"

The director nodded. "As you can see, I'm in way over my head. And so is Felix."

They both looked over at producers Felix Melvin and Jay Bergman, who were deep into a serious discussion.

"Goodness," said Nesta, trying to take it all in. "I can't believe this is your first film."

Victor finished his drink and prepared to leave the table. "Unfortunately," he said. "This will probably be my last."

Before he could leave, Nesta tried to get one last question in. "Wait! I've been dying to ask — how are you going to shoot the rest of Debbie Backes' scenes? Do you have a double or a stand-in?"

Victor looked at her in disbelief. "The *rest* of her scenes? Haven't you heard? We're having to shoot her scenes all over again."

Nesta couldn't contain her shock. "*Again*? *All* of them?!"

It pained the director to answer. "Every... single... one."

"But how? And with who?"

"We already have a new leading actor," said Victor. "She's flying in today from the US."

"From America?"

Before the director could elaborate any further, a woman burst into the dining room with a large entourage at her side. The hall went silent, and every person turned to look at her, as she removed her enormous sunglasses.

"Jay?!" she called out in a thick, Californian accent. "Jay? Where are you, my darling? I have come to save the day!"

Jay Bergman leapt to his feet and went running over to greet his new star.

Nesta turned back to Victor with a shocked face. "Is that really who I think it is?"

Victor nodded. "Yep. I'm afraid so. Things are about to get very interesting."

CHAPTER 14

"Bella Marsh?" asked Darren, chewing on his steak. "Who's that?"

Nesta had always taught her pupils that there was no such thing as a silly question, but she was prepared to make an exception on this occasion. "Are you serious? You've never heard of *Bella Marsh*?" She shook her head. "Your generation never ceases to amaze me."

Darren waited for his answer and wondered if it was ever going to come. He looked over at the woman in her large coat that everyone appeared to be staring at. She was now sitting at the producer's table and hadn't stopped talking since she arrived. "Is she a politician or something?"

Nesta sighed and couldn't bear the cultural ignorance any longer. "Bella Marsh was an American film icon. She used to be in all the thrillers during the late seventies and early eighties."

"There's your first problem," said Darren. "You used the word — *was*. I don't know if you remember, but we're living in the *now*."

"Yes, alright. No need to get clever. It's not my fault they don't make good films anymore. No wonder Bella hasn't been around for a long time. In fact, it feels like she disappeared completely by the mid-nineties." Nesta could hear the actor's famous, high-pitched laugh. "Sounds like she's back with a vengeance."

Darren stared down at his steak and wished he'd specified "well-done". Why anyone would assume he wanted it cooked medium-rare he would never understand. But they weren't in his local gastro pub now. "They're really going to shoot the whole film again using an American?" he asked.

"I'm sure she'll be putting on an English accent," said Nesta.

"Then why not use someone English?"

Nesta gazed over at Bella's table. The producers were hanging on her every word, and it was as though Debbie Backes was a distant memory already. "It would seem that there's a lot of politics involved in this casting."

"Is everything alright for you?"

Nesta and Darren both looked up to see Leigh, their bearded waiter.

"It's lovely," said Nesta.

Leigh nodded and turned to her dining partner. "And how about you, sir?"

Darren stared at his piece of undercooked meat. "Got any ketchup?"

Nesta cringed and quickly tried to change the subject. "How is your head chef doing?" she asked.

The waiter stared at her, as though nobody (including himself) had ever expressed concern over the chef before. "Uh, he's okay, I guess."

"He seemed very down after the incident with the mash," Nesta said.

"Oh," said Leigh. "Yeah, that wasn't our finest hour." He looked around to make sure no one was listening. "To be honest, Billy is never really in a good mood, anyway. The guy's always a bit grumpy."

Nesta nodded and remembered what the chef had told her about his feelings towards the waiting staff. "I got that impression. Has there been much disruption with the police?"

Leigh's face lit up. His shifts at the hotel restaurant were normally quite repetitive, and the murder investigation had made everything a little more interesting. "They've already searched the kitchen. And we all got interviewed." He tilted up his head with a smug grin. "I told the detective everything I could. I'd thought about joining the police force myself, actually. I reckon I'd make a great detective."

"Don't we all," said Nesta, exchanging a knowing look with Darren. "Do you know what they were looking for? In the kitchen?"

"Well," said Leigh. "They say that actor was killed by a steak knife."

"Who are *they*?"

"You know — everyone. Word travels fast around this hotel. And that Backes woman was the most unpopular guest we've ever had. Nobody had a good word to say about her."

Nesta thought about the way Debbie had spoken with the hotel manager. If the woman was comfortable enough to berate the most senior member of the hotel staff, she could only imagine what it was like for the staff at the lower end of the food chain. "What made her so unpopular?"

The waiter scoffed. "She treated this place like her own house. She arrived weeks before the rest of her crew. Probably trying to milk all the expenses she could. We didn't even know who she was at first. I don't watch soaps, and a lot of my colleagues don't either." He let out a sly grin. "I think she hated the fact that none of us recognised her. We get a lot of people like her staying at this hotel. They think they have some kind of power over us. Like we're terrified of losing our jobs. But this

Backes woman was a whole other level. She even got one person sacked."

His last detail caused a ripple of intrigue across the table. Nesta and Darren both looked at each other.

"Yeah," Leigh continued. "She was a right piece of work. We were all fuming."

Nesta turned to him and asked the next obvious question: "Who did she get sacked?"

"Our night manager, Benny."

"You have a night manager?"

"Not right now. Our general manager's still trying to find a replacement. That's why he's a bit stressed at the moment. He's having to do Benny's job as well."

"I imagine a murder investigation probably doesn't help," said Nesta.

"Oh, yes. That, too. He can be a bit of a drama queen, Elliott. He doesn't suit his job. That's why all the staff used to love Benny. The guy's been working the night shifts for years, but he was considered Elliott's right-hand man. He was an actor, actually. That's why he worked at night. So he could do auditions and acting jobs during the day. The guy practically didn't sleep. That's probably why he went a bit nuts."

"Nuts?" Darren asked.

"He was a really chilled boss, but I think the lack of sleep affected his mental health. That's why he drank so much. We all knew he was drinking on the job, but when you're working the night shift, nobody really notices. You get away with strange behaviour because the day staff have gone home and most of the guests are asleep."

"Where does Debbie Backes fit into all this?" asked Nesta.

Leigh smiled. "That was the problem. Debbie Backes never seemed to sleep. I think she had insomnia. Which was not good for Benny."

Nesta could see where this was going. Personally, she had never had trouble sleeping. In fact, her late husband used to say that she could sleep anywhere — including "the Blitz," he would always say. Morgan, on the other hand, had been the lightest sleeper she had ever met. Even her breathing would stop him from falling asleep. The local police officer had also done his fair share of night shifts over the course of his career, and they probably hadn't helped his ability to fall asleep quickly. "I take it that Benny's shifts were not very quiet with Debbie around."

The waiter laughed. "He used to tell me that she was a nightmare. She'd call for him almost every hour. There was always something wrong, or she would need something specific. I think Benny's patience grew thin, and Debbie could sense it. All the staff loved working with Benny so much that we often covered for his mistakes. But one of the night shift workers said that Debbie caught Benny drinking on the job."

"How?" Darren asked. "He can't have made it *that* obvious."

Leigh shrugged. "I'm not surprised. Debbie was always wandering around this hotel in her dressing gown. Someone once caught her rummaging around in the kitchen trying to find a bottle opener."

"Why didn't she ask for one?" asked Nesta.

"Sometimes she'd take matters into her own hands to make a point. So that she could complain about how rubbish our service was."

Nesta was beginning to question whether Debbie had been of sound mind before she died and would not have been surprised if she wasn't. "Did she report the night manager for his drinking?"

Leigh let out a grave sigh. "She was a lot more cruel than that. A few of us met up with Benny for a drink after he was sacked. It turns out that Debbie was basically blackmailing him, emotionally. She turned him into her personal slave. There was nothing he could do about it. She could get him sacked in an instant if she said anything, and she knew that *he* knew." The waiter paused to prepare for his favourite part of the story. "But, eventually, one day, Benny finally cracked. He went absolutely nuts on her — screamed in her face, calling her every name under the sun, threatening her. She'd properly broken him. He completely lost it. Like anyone would with so little sleep."

"What did Debbie say?" asked Darren, who was enjoying every moment.

"She revealed a dictaphone. She'd recorded the entire thing. Apparently, she always carried one with her to record her conversations with staff members. To cover her back, I guess. Sounds like something she would do." Leigh nodded. "And that was that. Benny was caught bang to rights."

Nesta sat back in her chair. It would take her a moment to digest all of the information (as well as her food). "You mentioned that this night manager *threatened* her. Did he threaten to —"

"Threaten to — what?" Leigh saw the concerned expression on her face and nodded. He was about to confirm her gravest suspicion. "Kill her?"

CHAPTER 15

"Are you sure that's how she was?" Darren asked, lowering his mobile phone.

Nesta was lying on the floor beside her bed in a highly awkward position. "Yes! This is *exactly* how I found her. Do you think this is comfortable?" She heard a loud clicking noise as she readjusted her leg. That sound was never good, she thought to herself.

Darren shook his head in disbelief. "That's the weirdest position for a dead body I've ever seen," he muttered.

"And how many dead bodies *have* you seen, exactly?" asked Nesta with another click. "Because I can guarantee that I've seen two more than you."

"How many have you seen?"

"Two!"

The teenager stopped his recording. He couldn't have the sound of them bickering on his channel, not if he wanted people to take him seriously. "I've seen dead people in films and TV loads of times. Nobody's ever looked like they're trying to do yoga."

Nesta groaned as she sat herself up. "We're talking about a

human body that's as limp as a bag of carrots. It's not meant to look pretty. People collapse in all sorts of positions."

"Didn't you say that she was in a dressing gown?" asked Darren, plonking himself down on the side of the bed.

"Oh, yes!" Nesta began scanning the room for her complimentary robe. "Did you want me to put one on?"

Darren waved his hand. "That really won't be necessary. I can use my imagination. Besides, I doubt you want to get a fine for staining the carpet with a bottle full of ketchup."

Nesta looked down at the clean floor and nodded. "That's a good point."

They both gazed around the room and tried to picture the scene of the crime.

"So the door wasn't locked?" asked Darren.

"It was open when I walked in. But that's because the staff member was already in there — the one who screamed. She said it was also left ajar when *she* arrived, and she called out a few times before she walked in with the gin and tonic. That's when she found her. Debbie's hair was wet, so it was clear she'd just had a shower."

"Who has a bath or a shower in the evening? I've never understood that."

Nesta's face went slightly pink, and she coughed. "I happened to be in the bath at the time. Without the gin and tonic, sadly."

"You were having a bath?" Darren asked.

"I was on holiday," Nesta snapped, slightly more defensively than she had intended. "I had to come running in my towel."

The teenager tried not to picture that part too much and steered the conversation back to Debbie Backes. "The killer must have been in a real hurry."

"What makes you say that?"

"They didn't even bother to close the door behind them.

Surely you would pause to close it, but this person didn't bother." He paused and glanced over towards the bathroom door. "Unless they were still in the room when you and the staff member were there."

Nesta felt a cold chill and saw that he was looking at the bathroom. "No, impossible. Shortly after I found the body, two more guests came into the room. The body was never left alone until the police arrived."

"Who were these other two people?"

"One was the prop master and the other was Jane Redman, the other actor. It makes sense because both of their rooms are across the hall."

Darren frowned. "What took them so long?"

"How do you mean?" Nesta asked back.

"You got there pretty quickly. If their rooms were nearby, then what took them so long?"

Nesta shrugged. "I have pretty quick reflexes. Even when I'm relaxing." She ignored the teenager's cynical stare and headed over to the door. "So these doors lock when they shut. And we can be pretty sure that it was locked whilst Debbie was having a shower. There were no bloodstains across the carpet, so we know she wasn't stabbed in the bathroom. Either the killer was let in, or they had a second room key."

Darren was still sitting at the edge of the bed, trying to keep up. He could see that Nesta was proud of her thorough detective work, and they were both becoming quite proficient at navigating these vicious crimes (or at least *he* thought they were, anyway).

"So what you're basically saying," he said, "is that it could have been anyone in this whole building?"

Nesta paused to give it some thought. "Yes, I suppose it could be." After a disappointed sigh, she could be certain of one thing — it was time for bed.

Darren had never heard snoring like it. Nesta's bed was a decent number of feet away from his own (if a sleeping bag rolled over a sofa could be described as a bed), and, still, the teenager could hear those loud noises as if she were lying beside him. He spent at least an hour trying to distract himself from the snores by covering his ears with headphones and streaming a number of videos on his phone. Even a *Deathdemons* music video had not been enough to compete with his fellow room-mate, and he eventually decided to leave the room altogether in search of a midnight snack.

He had never been a good sleeper and was often forced to find strange and creative ways to drift off at night. Sometimes an empty stomach was enough to keep him awake, and, having barely eaten his evening meal down in the dining room, he was ready to remedy his hunger problem with a big bowl of *Dorritos*. It didn't have to be *Dorritos*, of course. Any type of crisp would do (it wasn't like he was fussy) — even though the young man did consider himself somewhat of a crisp connoisseur.

"Are you alright, sir?"

Hotel manager Elliott Ball was standing behind the front reception desk, when he noticed one of his guests aimlessly wandering through the lobby.

Darren was on his way to the dining room and paused to acknowledge the intrigued man. "Just looking to get something to eat. I'm starving."

Elliott studied the teenager's appearance and squinted his disapproving eyes. He knew this young man's type and contained a few of them on his staff roster. They never lasted long, and he had developed a natural dislike of anyone below the age of twenty-five. None of them seemed to take any pride in their work, unlike him, who had been forced to slave his way to the top.

"The kitchen's closed," he said.

A confused Darren glanced in the direction of the dining hall. "Oh. Well, that's a bit rubbish. Why do they bother making you work at this time? Surely, we don't need a receptionist at night."

The man behind the desk began grinding his teeth. "I'll have you know I'm the general manager of this hotel."

"You are?" Darren asked, not in the slightest bit fazed. "Problem sorted, then. You can send yourself home."

"I'm working because we currently don't have an experienced night manager," Elliott snapped, before realising that he didn't need to explain himself to *this* obnoxious young man.

"You need experience to be a night manager?" Darren leant himself against the counter and chuckled. "Surely anyone with enough caffeine can stand around all night."

The hotel manager wasn't prepared to be lured into an argument, and he took a deep sigh. "Is there anything else I can help you with, sir?"

Darren checked his watch. "Reckon there's anywhere still open with something to eat? Like a petrol station or something? They normally do good pasties."

Elliott scoffed. "It's only ten o'clock. I'm sure there will be *somewhere* in the city of Chester that can oblige."

"Nice one," said Darren. He hesitated before walking away. "Am I supposed to tip you for that or something?"

The hotel manager glared at him. "That won't be necessary."

Moments later, and the teenager was walking the streets like a lost puppy. The young man from Bala had only visited the city a couple of times, but usually with his father and never at night. Chester became like most other urban environments at this late hour and had a sense of mystery lurking in those dark shadows and quiet alleyways.

Darren eventually found himself on the more lively side of town, where bars and restaurants appeared to be still thriving. He suddenly felt an overwhelming feeling of loneliness, as he heard the cries and laughter of people socialising in their small groups. Judging by the sight of these artisan eateries with their stylish decors and retro lighting, it was unlikely he would find his deep-filled pasty on *this* street anytime soon.

Once he had reached the end of Watergate Street, he had no choice but to turn around and head back.

"Hey! Iron Maiden!"

Darren froze. The last time someone had called him that, he was walking through a school corridor. Surely his archnemesis from Bala hadn't followed him all the way to Chester.

He turned and saw two adults sitting around a table outside a small bar. He recognised one of them from the hotel dining hall and saw him pointing towards his Iron Maiden t-shirt.

Sound designer Jezza and his boom operator, Maddie, were both puffing away on their cigarettes. Both appeared to be heavy metal enthusiasts themselves and featured the names of two other rock legends on their own shirts.

"*Iron Maiden!*" Jezza called out again, stroking a beard so long it would make every member of *ZZ Top* jealous. "You look lost!"

Darren saw the bowl of chips on their table and crossed the street to join them. "I'm looking for something to eat," he said. "Where did you get them?"

Jezza watched him point at his bowl and laughed. "Grab a seat and help yourself. We've barely touched them, anyway. Eating's cheating in my book."

Maddie blew out a puff of smoke and pointed to the man's midriff. "You wouldn't know it to look at you."

The large man laughed and patted his stomach with pride. "Yeah, you've got me there. Keeps me warm at night, though."

"It's the only company at night you'll ever get," Maddie muttered.

Jezza howled again and turned to the teenager. "Can you believe her? I'm supposed to be her boss!"

Darren smiled, as the woman thumped her sound designer on the arm. The tattoos running up her sleeveless arms caught the teenager's curious eye and made him slightly envious. She seemed like she could have the man beside her for breakfast if she wanted to and had the slender physique of a light-heavyweight boxer.

"Whoever said that the sound designer's in charge?" she asked. "I'm the one who does all the recording."

"The grunt work," said Jezza, bravely. "I'm the brains — you're the brawn."

Maddie scoffed.

"Are you the boom operator?" Darren asked.

Maddie tried not to appear offended. "I use many tools to record my sound. Not just the boom."

Jezza shrugged. "And, yet, either way, nobody can hear a thing."

Darren watched him receive another thump, whilst he stuffed a handful of chips into his mouth.

"Steady," said Maddie, noticing the teenager's large appetite. "You're like you haven't eaten in days."

"I wasn't keen on my hotel food," Darren mumbled.

"Tell me about it," said Jezza. "Why can't they just serve a normal steak and chips?"

"Cause the hotel manager's got a giant stick up his backside," said Maddie.

The teenager smiled. He was beginning to like his new dining partners. "He doesn't seem very happy in his job."

"Who? The hotel manager?" Jezza sniggered. "He's the biggest plonker I've ever met. He didn't even know where his maintenance room was."

"What did *you* want with a maintenance room?" asked Maddie.

"Needed a spanner to adjust the pressure in my shower."

"Since when were you a plummer? Just ask the front desk."

Jezza folded up his arms in protest. "I fix everything myself in my house. Why should I do anything different in a hotel? They don't know what they're doing, anyway."

Maddie shook her head. "I'm not letting you anywhere near my plumbing. You're the clumsiest, noisest sound designer I've ever met. I should have you banned from the set. I'm not surprised the hotel manager didn't want you anywhere near the maintenance room."

Darren watched them both bicker for another ten minutes. "I told the guy he should get some sleep."

"He's a strange bloke, that manager," said Maddie, blowing smoke into the air as she pondered Elliott's behaviour over the last few days. "I caught him sneaking onto set a couple of times."

"He's one of those creepy autograph hunters," said Jezza. "The guy asked me to get Debbie Backes to sign his photograph. Don't know why he thought *I'd* be any help. The woman barely acknowledged me. I fitted radio microphones to her on five different occasions, and she acted like I wasn't there."

"Rather you than me," said Maddie with a shudder. "I hate fitting radio mics on people. Those actors always make it awkward."

"Was the hotel manager really that fussed about getting an autograph?" asked Darren, who had only really heard of people getting selfies. Why anyone would want a signature on a piece of paper he could never understand (unless you worked in a bank).

"He's apparently a huge Debbie Backes fan," said Jezza. "He

must have been over the moon when he found out that she was coming to stay at the hotel. Although, Debbie *was* very selective with her autographs. She didn't dish them out to anyone."

"I guess there's no chance of him getting one from her now," said Maddie with a wry smile. "Unless he forces one out from her cold, dead hand. I can imagine him doing that, too, the weirdo."

Darren continued to devour his chips, whilst he listened to the pair discuss the technical complications of their unusual trade. They had experienced a difficult shoot so far and were apprehensive about what the next few weeks would have in store for them.

"I can't believe we're starting again," Maddie muttered.

"Only the Barbara Madden scenes," said Jezza.

"Which is almost all of them! Debbie was the main character."

"More money for us." The sound designer raised his glass. "If the production company is happy to waste their money on re-shoots, then I'm more than happy to take it." He turned to the teenager. "How about, young man? Fancy a career in the film and television business? Getting paid a fortune for doing bugger all?"

"Speak for yourself," snapped Maddie.

"I'm already in the business," said Darren. The other two stared at him, until he looked up and noticed their surprise. "I've got my own online video channel."

The two sound specialists turned to look at each other with an amused smile.

"Is that right?" asked Jezz. "What videos you got on there? People falling over? Cats making funny noises?"

"It's a true crime channel." Darren spoke with such confidence that it only amused his listeners even more.

"True crime?" Jezz slammed his large hand against the table

and laughed. "Now I was not expecting *that* one! How many followers you got, Jake Paul? Your mum and dad?"

"A couple of thousand," said Darren. "But it's growing, and the views are strong. The channel's called *The D&N Files*."

"Hey!" Maddie cried. "I watch that channel." Her words completely wiped the smile from Jezza's face.

"You — what?" he asked in disbelief.

"That's the one with that retired Welsh teacher who goes around covering random murder cases," Maddie continued. "It popped up in my feed a couple of months ago. I love true crime."

Darren couldn't hide his enjoyment. "That's the one! I'm the one who started it. It's why I'm in Chester."

"No way!" Maddie raised her hand and gave him a high-five, all whilst her colleague just remained speechless. "That's cool. Hey! You could cover that Debbie Backes mu —" She paused and nodded. "Right, that's why you're here. You guys work fast."

"Helps when my associate's already in town," said Darren. "She tends to attract murders for some reason."

"Maybe because she's the killer!" Maddie cried with a laugh.

Jezza tried to get the other two members of his group's attention. "Wait, are you telling me you've really got a viral video channel?"

Darren shrugged. "I wouldn't say viral just yet. But it's growing." He placed the last chip in his mouth. "You two just do sound, though, right? No camera work."

His question ignited the bearded man into a defensive frenzy. "*Just* sound? Are you kidding? We're the most important part! Have you tried watching a film without any sound? Watched an action sequence without any audio effects? Nobody jumps in a horror film because of the camera work — it's because of the sound!"

"Chill out," said Maddie, patting the excitable man on the

back. "He wasn't trying to offend us. The lad knows how important sound is, right?" She turned to the teenager with a glare.

"Oh, yeah! Sure…" Darren cleared his throat. "Sound and camerawork are, like, fifty-fifty, right?"

A sulking Jezza stared at him. "I'd say it's more like eighty-twenty in our favour."

"Stop being an old dinosaur," said Maddie. She turned back to Darren with the excitement of a superfan. "Hey! You could feature me on your channel!"

"You?" asked Jezza. "What makes you think he wants a video of you?"

"Because I'm a key witness."

The table went silent.

Maddie smiled. She enjoyed making them wait to find out more. "Yeah, that's right. I'm one of the first people the police interviewed."

"You never told me that," said Jezza.

"We're not a married couple, you know? There's a lot about me that I haven't told you about."

"What exactly did you see?" asked Darren. He was a little cynical, having been aware that Nesta had found the body. Unless she had witnessed the actual murder taking place, then he was convinced that the woman knew very little.

"I saw someone fleeing the scene of the crime," said Maddie, rather proud of herself.

"What did he look like?"

"It was a woman," Maddie snapped. "I thought it was Debbie at first, as she had similar clothes and similar hair, although it was a different colour. Debbie was a brunette, but this person had red hair. She was wearing a striped, black and yellow dress with a bright-green cardigan over the top. Strange mix — red trainers, too. I was heading down the hallway when I saw her come running out of Debbie's room. She ran off up the hall before I got a proper look at her."

"When was this?" asked Darren. He had learnt from Nesta that timings were everything in a case like this, especially in a building full of people.

"It was about five or ten minutes before her body was found. I didn't think anything of it at the time. But obviously that changed when I heard about the murder."

Their table went silent again. Darren's mind was whirling, and he couldn't wait to tell Nesta. Unfortunately, she was probably still fast asleep, and he would have to wait until morning. If the teenager thought that he had trouble sleeping *before*, then he was in for a long night. His newfound information would keep his brain ticking away for at least a few more hours, yet.

He was just about to bid the two sound engineers a short goodnight, when Darren noticed a man stumbling down the street. Billy, *The Legion Hotel's* seasoned head chef, was still dressed in his whites, which were now covered in large stains of blood.

CHAPTER 16

"Sounds like you had quite the night," said Nesta. She was sitting back against the head rest of her king-sized bed with a cup of complimentary tea in her hand.

Darren was still wrapped in his sleeping bag and spread out across the uncomfortable sofa. His bad night's sleep had given him a permanent scowl, and he wriggled like a slug to find a more bearable position. "I wasn't out that long."

"Enough to discover an important piece of evidence." Nesta sipped on her hot tea. She had been impressed with the teenager's findings and had already been meaning to speak with Maddie about her interview with the detective. Now they had another witness. "Did you find out why that chef got into a scuffle?"

Darren shook his head. He had filled her in about the curious sighting of Billy and his stained work clothes. It turned out that the head chef had been drinking heavily that night and found himself embroiled in a vicious pub brawl. "He said he'd got into an argument with a complete stranger at the bar. One thing led to another."

Nesta shook her head. "It always does." She stretched out

her arms and yawned. "I feel nice and refreshed now. I think I've had some of the best night's sleep I've ever had in this bed."

"How nice for you," Darren muttered, rubbing his sore back.

"Right!" Nesta cried out. "That's enough lounging about. We've got a busy day ahead of us."

"We *have*?" Darren was eyeing up her comfy bed and had a right mind to stay in the hotel room all day.

Nesta jumped to her feet and threw on her dressing gown. "I have it on good authority that they're shooting a scene at the racecourse today."

"Oh, goody." The teenager covered up his tired head with the help of his hoodie. "How exciting..."

"Yes," said Nesta. "Isn't it? I've always loved the Chester racecourse. And there should be a few crowd shots. They'll need plenty of extras. Maybe I'll get to dress up in one of those nice hats!" She did a giddy dance and scurried across the room. "I'll have a shower first, then, shall I?"

Darren responded with a groan and buried himself underneath his pillow.

LOCATED on the banks of the River Dee, Chester Racecourse held the proud title of being the oldest racecourse still in operation and hosted many prestigious events throughout the year. Nesta had never been interested in horse racing, but she could appreciate the excitement of a *Grand National* or an *Epsom Derby* — not to mention the historical significance of the venue itself. According to her pamphlet, Chester Racecourse had once acted as a Roman harbour during the city's settlement, a fun fact that the teenager beside her was not remotely interested in.

"Will you cheer up?" she asked, as they walked along the

grassy terrain of the empty race track. "You've been miserable all morning. Look where we are!"

Darren watched her do a little twirl with her arms raised up in the air. "That's easy for you to say when you've had a full night's rest."

"Well, maybe you should go to bed earlier." Nesta's remark was met with a huff, and she continued their tour of the grounds. "There they are, look!" She pointed upwards in the direction of one of the stands, where the entire film crew were busy setting up.

"I thought you said there was going to be crowds of extras," said Darren.

Nesta saw what he was referring to and pulled a concerned face. There were only a handful of people dressed in Victorian clothes, and the viewing stands beside them were all empty. "Maybe we're early," she said.

The crew members were all frantically running around when she approached the small set, and she spotted their silent director, lurking about in the background. "There you are," she said, cornering him whilst she still could. "Do you need any more extras?"

Victor gave her his usually distant look. "Hmh? Oh, you're asking the wrong person. You'll have to speak with the second-AD."

"The — who?"

"Second AD. Second assistant director. They normally handle the extras. But I think we've got enough people."

Nesta took another look around. There were only eight people dressed in period-drama clothing, and, as far as she was aware, this was quite a poor turnout for a horse race.

"Are you sure?" she asked. "I believe that this racecourse holds at least two thousand people."

Victor scoffed. "Do you know how expensive that would be?

We're shooting this scene really tight on the actors. We only need people to fill the edges of the frame. The wide shot of the crowds will all be done digitally in post-production."

A disappointed Nesta merely stared at him. She understood very little of what was coming out of the man's mouth, but she knew it meant that her first film cameo would have to wait.

The director could see her confusion, and he smiled. "Oh, yeah. There's no expense spared on this production. If there's a way to cut corners, we will. Especially now that we're having to start again with our precious leading lady. Talking of which… looks like her majesty has arrived."

They looked over to see Bella Marsh and her entourage heading through the main gates, followed by a group of security people.

"I wish I attracted that much attention when I arrive to set," said Oliver Nash.

Nesta turned around to see that the actor was now standing behind her with a jealous expression. "Careful what you wish for," she said. "I'm sure it gets old very quickly."

Oliver shook his head. "That's just what people who aren't famous say. Only a small percentage of the population get to experience that feeling."

"Being recognised everywhere you go?" asked Nesta. "Having people stop you in the supermarket every five minutes?" She paused, suddenly, and realised that she was describing her own life back in Bala. Perhaps she *did* know what fame felt like, she thought. When you lived in a town where everyone knew your name, there was no need to chase even more attention.

"Even Debbie Backes wasn't Bella-Marsh-famous," Oliver continued. "Although, she acted like she was."

"She's not proper famous," said Darren. "I still don't know who Ella Mars is."

"You see," said Nesta, turning to the fame-hungry actor. "You can never be famous enough. There will always be someone more famous than you are in this world." She paused to re-consider. "Except maybe the King of England or something. And even then —" She turned to Darren and put on her old teacher-voice. "Can you tell me the name of the King of England?"

Darren pulled a disinterested face. "Don't really care."

"There," said Nesta. "He's proved my point. Fame is a dangerous pursuit. It will never be enough to make you happy."

Oliver chuckled. She had still not convinced him. "I'll come back to you when I'm rich and famous. If I'm still not happy by that point — at least I'm rich and famous."

Even Darren struggled not to be amused and let out a laugh. "He's got a point there."

Nesta shook her head. "Don't say I didn't warn you. Wait until this film comes out. You'll be mobbed in the street."

"*This* film?" Oliver asked. "I think it's safe to say that this film is more likely to kill my career stone dead. It was bad enough being in a film with Debbie Backes. Now I've got a yank trying to play an English Victorian. This film is going to bomb — *badly*."

"I'll still watch it," said Nesta with her head held high.

"There she is!" cried an American voice. "Bore da! Is that how you say it?"

Jay Bergman was flashing his whitened teeth like an excited horse.

"Very good," said Nesta, cringing as he placed a hand on her shoulder. A confused Darren and Oliver both looked at each other.

"It's in the blood," said Jay. "Oh! And I've found you the perfect part. You're going to love it!"

Suddenly, Nesta didn't mind his disregard for her personal space, and her eyes lit up. "Have you *really*? I can be an extra?"

"Not just an extra." Jay clapped his hands. "I even got you a line!"

Nesta felt her knees go weak. "I have to say something?"

"Just a few words. But I know you're gonna nail it! The Welsh have a good track record on the silver screen: Richard Burton, Anthony Hopkins, Catherine Zeta-Jones..."

Darren chuckled. "You're comparing her to Catherine Zeta-Jones?"

"Don't listen to him," said Nesta. "He's not the brightest lad, I'm afraid. I think it's all that time watching Tok-Tic videos. Kills off the brain cells."

Darren frowned, as the other men laughed.

Oliver didn't bother to hide his disapproval of Jay's offer. "You know how long it took for me to get a line of dialogue? Three years of drama school, countless auditions and a load of dodgy adverts!"

Jay patted the young actor on the back. "Wait until you hit sixty, kid. Most actors have either quit the business or given up long before. The parts come flying in."

"Whoever said I was over sixty?" Nesta asked. "How rude!"

The producer held up his arms in defence and quickly tried to change the subject. "So, Mr Nash! Is that a stage name by the way?"

Oliver frowned. "No. That's my real name."

Jay shrugged and placed an arm around his supporting actor. "You ready to knock this one out of the park, or what? I hear you've got some big credentials, Mr *RADA*."

"Well," said Oliver with a gulp. "It all depends on my co-star. It takes two to make a strong performance. I did ask Bella for a rehearsal, but she knocked me back."

Jay raised his eyebrow. "Rehearsal? Are you kidding? You know how much Bella costs? I pay you actors to get it right the first time, kid." He let out a laugh and gave the young man a squeeze. "What was it Hitchcock said? All actors are like cattle? Something like that. But he was right. You're my prized livestock, buddy. And I expect big things. You go find us some of that so-called chemistry." He lowered his voice for a moment. "And I'll be straight with you here and say that chemistry was severely lacking during your scenes with Debbie Backes. I'm sure you'll agree."

Oliver went pale and his usual confidence slipped away for a moment. "I didn't think —"

"I don't pay you to think, Mr Nash — I pay you to act!" The producer shook him again and sniggered. "Don't look so upset, kid. I'm giving you a second chance here. You ever heard of director notes? Well, here are some for free. Now go break a leg! You're gonna be terrific."

The producer swaggered off and left the confused actor lost for words.

"Are you alright?" Nesta asked him.

Oliver Nash swallowed an enormous gulp. "I think I'll be fine."

CHAPTER 17

The racecourse scene had not gone entirely to plan. Despite his small panic attack, Oliver Nash had managed to scrape through by the skin of his teeth. What should have been a straightforward dialogue scene had felt more complex than a choreographed fight sequence. A sudden bout of unexpected rain showers had only made matters worse, and the already ropey camerawork was exacerbated further by some of the most inconsistent lighting that the continuity person had ever encountered.

Nevertheless, the most surprising blunder of the entire morning had been the long-awaited performance of the production's new lead actor.

"Did you hear her accent?" asked Darren, as he and Nesta made their leisurely stroll back along the river. "I thought she was supposed to be English."

The teenager was right, Nesta thought. Bella's dialogue had sounded like a cross between a West Country accent and a *Monty Python* sketch. And the entire crew seemed to have noticed, including their distraught director. American producer Jay Bergman, on the other hand, had found her performance "marvellous" and didn't seem to have much of an ear for authentic British accents.

"Maybe this film really is doomed," said Nesta, watching a boat with the name Mark Twain along the side cruise past.

"I don't know why they don't just pull the plug and make an action film instead," said Darren.

"There's too much at stake. Although, it makes me wonder how much of the production's bad luck is down to chance."

Darren smiled. "You think someone is trying to sabotage the film on purpose? Who would want to do that?"

"Who knows. But it all looks a bit suspicious to me." Nesta thought again about the sighting outside of Debbie Backes' room. "We really need to find out who that person was, fleeing the scene of the crime. Maddie said that she looked similar to Debbie."

"Did Debbie Backes have a stunt double?" asked Darren. He always liked the idea of performing stunts on a film set and had not ruled it out as a viable career option. During the many hours of skateboarding on his makeshift park back in Bala, he had often filmed himself trying out a daring trick that usually ended in a fall.

"It's not really that kind of film," said Nesta. "But it's not a bad idea. Maybe there's a double for challenging movements like running or heading up staircases or something. That can't be easy for a person of Debbie's age when you're doing multiple takes."

Darren was quite happy with the words "not a bad idea". It was the closest he had come to a compliment so far and took it as a pat on the back. "We'll have to ask the crew. If there *is* a stunt double, they'll be staying at the hotel."

"Did you get any footage today?" asked Nesta. "For the channel?"

The teenager shook his head. "I got told to stop filming.

They probably don't want the public to see how bad their film is going to be."

Nesta shrugged. "That's a bit harsh. All publicity is good publicity."

"What I really need are some interviews from the hotel staff," said Darren. "We could have them all giving their account of the night Debbie Backes was killed. That way, even if we don't manage to find out who killed her, the viewers can make their own mind up. I saw them do it once on this documentary about a small Australian town. This guy goes missing, and the whole town becomes a suspect. Only there's a population of like ten people. They never found out who did it, but you can make a pretty good guess. I reckon it was the guy who owned a crocodile in his backgarden."

Nesta shuddered. "I'm glad there are no crocodiles in Bala."

They headed away from the river side and made the short walk back to their hotel. The dark rain clouds that had troubled the morning's shoot had completely vanished, and the sun was shining once again.

"Do you think the staff will agree to be interviewed?" asked Darren.

Nesta saw a number of film crew members heading towards *The Legion*'s grand entrance. "It's not just the staff I'm worried about." She let out a sigh and noticed Malcolm greeting his guests over in the distance. "But I'm sure we can persuade a few volunteers."

Darren saw who she was looking at and smirked. "You know that doorman fancies you?"

His question caught the woman by complete surprise, and she began stumbling on her own words. "I — don't — excuse me? Don't be so daft!"

The teenager continued to smile at her. "I saw the way you two were looking at each other yesterday." He placed his hands together and formed a heart. "Don't pretend you haven't noticed."

Nesta watched him begin kissing the air and *whacked* him with her tourist brochure. "Stop that — right now! Shame on you. The man's just trying to do his job."

"Whatever you say," said Darren.

"Ah, Nesta!" Malcolm gave his favourite guest a wave and strolled over in his long coat. "How are we?"

Darren gave Nesta a knowing look, and she shook her head. "Malcolm! How nice to see you."

The doorman chuckled. "It's not like you can miss me. I'm never far from this front door." He tipped his hat at Darren. "Young man. I hope your grandmother has given you a good tour of the city."

"Of course," said Nesta, before the teenager could answer. "I've made sure to cover all of the sights. We've just come back from the racecourse."

Malcolm's face lit up. "The racecourse! Ah, how I love the racecourse. Lost plenty of money down there in my time." The man chuckled and turned back to Darren. "Hey! I should introduce you to my nephew. You two youngsters would get on like a house on fire."

Nesta enjoyed watching Darren's face cringe, as the doorman summoned the reluctant porter over. "Henry! Henry!!"

After finally putting his mobile phone away, Henry dragged himself up from the suitcase he'd been sitting on.

"How many times have I told you to put that thing away when you're working," Malcolm snapped, as he approached. "And you could at least stand up and try to look professional." Henry refused to acknowledge his criticism and merely yawned. "Did you want something?"

Malcolm turned to Nesta with an eye roll. "You can't find the staff these days." He pointed at Darren. "This is my nephew, Henry. Henry, this is —"

"Darren..."

"Darren! That's it."

The two young men stared at each other like two neighbouring house cats who had been forced into a room together.

"Alright," said Darren.

"Alright," said Henry.

Nesta and Malcolm decided to escape the awkward atmosphere and move away.

"Like two peas in a pod," said Nesta.

"Yes, quite." The doorman shook his head. "I do worry about that generation. How they'll ever communicate without the use of those gadgets, I'll never know."

Nesta nodded. "I'm sure they'll invent microchips or something for those overstimulated brains of theirs."

Malcolm laughed. "You have the mind of a twisted scientist, Nesta. Shame on you."

"Don't worry. Science was never my strongest subject, so there's no chance of me inventing anything like that. I can barely operate the microwave at home."

They both turned to see that Darren and Henry were now staring at their mobile phone screens.

"Maybe they're telepathic," said Malcolm.

The doorman excused himself briefly to greet an approaching couple, and he returned as quickly as he could. "Sorry about that. Part of the job, I'm afraid."

"I notice you take a lot of pride in your work," said Nesta.

Malcolm straightened up his posture. "Absolutely. It's my duty. I've been doing this job my entire life."

"Some might say that you're the face of this hotel."

Nesta's compliment made the man blush. "Why, I've never thought of it that way before. Shame it's not a prettier face, eh?"

"Don't be silly," said Nesta, shoving him on the shoulder. "You have a wonderful face."

The doorman loosened his collar and let out a cough. Even Nesta didn't know where to look, having unintentionally created an awkward silence. "So," she said. "You must see a lot outside these doors. Plenty of people coming and going."

"Oh, yes." Malcolm was more than happy to discuss his work, seeing as he spent more time at the hotel than at home. "I really am the eyes and ears of this place. I like to think of myself as something of a protector. I'm not technically a security guard, you see. But the safety of our staff and guests is always at the forefront of my mind. I'll have no trouble going on here."

Nesta admired the man's physique. Regardless of his age, he was still tall and stocky, with broad shoulders that fit snugly into his coat. "You look like you could handle yourself quite well. Do you exercise?"

Malcolm laughed and patted his own stomach. "Sadly not. Although, I probably should. I've always been naturally big-boned. Just like my father. He never lifted a dumbbell in his life but was naturally big and strong." He tipped his hat. "We doormen are more of a concierge than a bouncer. But mark my words — if a person is up to no good, I'll be the first to chuck them out."

"I don't doubt it," said Nesta. "I'm sure this hotel is the safest in Chester."

The doorman grimaced. "It was until this dreadful actor business."

"You mean Debbie Backes?"

"Is that her name?" Malcolm asked. "I'm afraid I don't really get time to watch much television."

"Fortunately, I'm retired." Nesta smiled. "I've even got time for the repeats."

"Are you really retired? You don't seem old enough."

"Stop it," Nesta snapped. "I'm not falling for that one."

They both giggled.

"If it makes you feel any better," said Malcolm, "I should really be retired myself by now."

"Then why don't you?"

Nesta's question made the man uncomfortable. "Well, I don't know. Once you hit the retire-button, there's no going back then, is there? I'm afraid that I'll regret it."

"Nonsense," said Nesta. "People come out of retirement all the time. Take boxers for example. Floyd Mayweather retired when he was thirty-eight. Then came out of retirement at forty. Retirement's just a word."

"Are you really comparing me to a heavyweight boxer?" asked Malcolm, failing to hide his approval.

"I believe Floyd was a lightweight." Nesta paused to think about it. "Or was it light middleweight? I can never remember."

The man saw her cheeky smile and nodded. "And how about you? Do you regret retiring?"

"Not one bit. It's been an entirely new adventure. Like a second life."

"Oh? And what exactly have you been doing?"

Nesta shrugged. "Oh, the usual things that people do when they retire: travel around, solve crimes, get into trouble. That sort of thing."

Malcolm laughed. "Is that right? Sounds pretty fun to me. Maybe, I should consider it."

"You should," said Nesta. "Life's short. You need to take chances and seize every opportunity." She paused. "That's rich coming from me, but I'm getting better."

Her words struck a chord with the man, and he nodded. "Perhaps I should have come across you sooner in my life. I've never been much of a risk taker or chancer. Maybe that's why I never got married."

"You really think so?" asked Nesta. She saw the sadness in his eyes which made her want to give him a cuddle, but she had never been much of a hugger.

"I'm almost certain of it," said Malcolm. "They say love doesn't just come knocking on your door. You have to go out and find it. A big part of my job is waiting to greet people. Maybe I took that approach into my personal life as well. You can't just wait around forever."

"That sounds very wise."

Malcolm removed his hat and combed back his hair. "Yes, well. I'm not just a pretty face."

They both chuckled.

Nesta saw that the man had discussed his private life enough and decided to steer their conversation back to something a little lighter. Like murder. "So, have you spotted anyone suspicious walking through these doors?"

"Suspicious?"

"You must have come across every guest in this hotel, standing out here. Is there anyone who stands out?"

Malcolm gave her a surprised stare. "You weren't joking about the solving crimes part, were you?" He took a moment to think. "We've had plenty of unusual characters since this film lot arrived. Most of them are an odd bunch. It's like a travelling circus. But is there anyone capable of *murder*? I couldn't say just by looking at them for five seconds. They say even a serial killer can seem perfectly normal until you get to know them."

"What about your work colleagues?"

The doorman laughed before realising that she was being serious. "My fellow staff?" He shook his head. "Absolutely not. Take my own boss. He's the most cold-blooded man I've ever met, but there's no way he's capable of anything like that."

"The hotel manager?" asked Nesta.

Malcolm saw the curious look in her eye and immediately

regretted what he had just said. "No, no! I'm not for a moment suggesting that —"

"Your boss is a killer?" Nesta smiled. "I'm sure you wouldn't be the first. Or the last. My last headteacher was definitely a psychopath."

"You're going to get me into trouble if you're not careful," said Malcolm. He saw the mischief in her face and realised that he had never quite met a woman like Nesta before. She had an excitement about her, a sense of wonder and adventure that he was beginning to crave in his own life.

Nesta turned to Darren and his new friend, who still hadn't appeared to have said a word to each other the entire time. "Right," she said. "We'd better let these gentlemen get back to work." She bid the doorman and his nephew a farewell and headed towards the large doors. Just as she was about to walk inside, there was a gentle call. "Oh, Nesta!"

She turned around to see Malcom's nervous face. He summoned up a burst of courage and prepared to ask his burning question. "Would you fancy having dinner this week? Any evening would work."

The man was forced to wait the longest pause of his life, until Nesta smiled. "I'd love to."

CHAPTER 18

"You want to go to the gym?" Darren asked. The teenager was lying on the bed with a magazine in his hands when his roommate had broached the idea. He made himself quite at home in this luxurious hotel room and was currently being judged for having his dirty trainers on the freshly-prepared sheets.

"Why not?" asked Nesta, who was boiling the kettle and munching on a complimentary biscuit. "The gym and spa are all included. It would be daft not to."

Darren scoffed. "There's no way I'm stepping foot in a gym full of health freaks. Or a sauna full of naked blokes."

"Maybe it'll do us some good," said Nesta. She imagined herself in trendy gym gear, pumping iron and working up a sweat. If she was being honest, it sounded dreadful. But, like she had already said, it was all free, and she was determined to get her money's worth (even if it gave her a hernia). "It's important to look after ourselves, even at your age."

The teenager ripped open a bag of crisps and began chomping away whilst he spoke. "We've just walked all the way back from the racecourse. That's more steps than I've done in a month. I'd say we're all good. Besides, I'm on holiday."

Nesta's eyes widened. "Holiday? I thought you were supposed to be here on business. What about generating content for the channel?"

Darren stretched out his arms and yawned. "Work hard, play hard. That's my motto. There's no harm in having a break. Anyway, the content seems to generate itself in this hotel. Did you ask the doorman about getting an interview?"

"Uh, no." Nesta blushed. "It completely slipped my mind."

"What were you both talking about all that time, then?" asked Darren.

"I couldn't tell you. We were just chatting. It didn't feel like we were talking for that long."

The teenager sat up on the bed with a wicked grin on his face. "*Now* I know why you want to go to the gym!" He began posing like a young Arnold Schwarzenegger. "You want to get ripped for Mr Loverboy."

"Don't be so stupid!" Nesta snapped. She had a right mind to pour the boiled kettle over his entire head. "I'm very happy with the way I look, thank you very much. I stopped caring about what other people think a very long time ago. It's the wisdom that comes with age."

Darren shrugged. "Then I must be wise beyond my years. I don't care about my appearance either."

Nesta gazed down at his ripped jeans and tattered trainers. "I never said I didn't care about good dress sense. Or having a decent hair cut. Or good hygiene —"

"Alright!" Darren cried. "Don't go judging me! If you want to go hit the gym, be my guest. But I'm going to chill out and take it easy." He lifted up his headphones. "A bit of *Megadeth's Greatest Hits*. That's my stress relief."

Nesta rolled her eyes. "Well, don't say I didn't warn you when you're out of breath walking up the stairs."

"I'll take the escalator," Darren muttered. He had a sudden thought. "Oh, bring me back one of those sporty energy drinks, would you? I'm parched over here." The world went dark, as he felt a dirty towel land on his head.

THE LAST TIME Nesta had entered a gym, she had been looking for the toilet at *Bala Leisure Centre*. It wasn't that she was against an exercise routine (she had joined several classes in her time, including a weekly Zumba session headed by a local woman with two left feet), but the sterile environment of a room full of machines had never sat well with her. Nesta much preferred riding her bike in the great outdoors or walking her Jack Russell at the shores of her favourite lake.

The fitness room at *The Legion Hotel* was not that dissimilar to every other gym she had stepped foot in, although it was slightly more modern and stylish. Rather than being blinded by a ceiling full of harsh LED lights, she was greeted to a more serene environment with a neutral colour palette of deep greens and soft greys.

The music, on the other hand, had that same high-energy feel with a beat that thumped louder than Nesta's heart. This place had more in common with a nightclub, Nesta thought, only without any sign of a cocktail or sofa.

She took a deep breath and walked her way past a series of mysterious machines that resembled medieval torture devices with a stylish twist. There was one contraption that she at least recognised: a large running treadmill with more buttons than a starfleet cockpit.

Fortunately, Nesta had packed a pair of comfortable trainers (which had never travelled more than three miles-per-hour), and their rubber soles were soon touching the short, stationary conveyor belt.

After a few random clicks, she felt the ground beneath her finally begin to move, and she was forced to engage her legs into a light jog. Everything was going fine for the first thirty seconds, until Nesta heard a series of *beeps* which were accompanied by an increase in speed. A minute later, and she was moving into a full-on sprint, a speed that caused her to struggle to reach the controls. Things only got worse with more *beeps*, and she began contemplating a dive for safety.

"Help!" she cried out. "I can't stop it!"

Before her entire body gave in, a heroic hand came flying across the controls, and soon she was back to a steady walk. "Oh, thank goodness..." It took her a good couple of minutes to catch her breath back, and her heart rate was that of a person in the midst of a cardiac arrest. She had made a narrow escape from taking a perilous fall into the abyss and was eternally grateful to her kind saviour.

"What were you thinking?" asked a relieved Frida. The receptionist was dressed in her training gear and waited for the treadmill to come to a complete stop. "You had it set to Beast Mode."

Nesta was still trying to breathe and wiped the sweat pouring down from her red forehead. "*Beast Mode*? I never asked for *Beast Mode*! Back in my day, a treadmill had less than five buttons, and the only ones I ever used were *On* or *Off*!"

Frida smiled. "Maybe we need a cool down." She pointed to a pair of exercise bikes. "Care to join me for a light cycle? Great for active recovery after a hard workout."

Nesta was soon peddling away beside her new gym buddy. After a few minutes, she began huffing and puffing. "You call this a *cool down*?"

Frida reached across and adjusted some settings. "Just take it slow. It's not a race."

Nesta gazed around at the empty gym and sighed. She had never understood the idea of exerting so much energy whilst getting absolutely nowhere. The scenery had not changed one bit, and she was already bored out of her mind. "Do you really do this every day?" she asked.

"Most days," said Frida. "But I try to mix it up."

"By mixing it up, do you mean a nice brunch café?"

The receptionist chuckled. "I mean, I use different machines for different muscle groups. The body likes variety."

Nesta liked variety, too, but didn't equate that to more machines. "You must be very fit. No wonder you won all those competitions."

"I don't train anywhere near the amount that I used to," said Frida. "But when you sit behind a counter all day like me, you have to do *something*."

"Ladies!" a voice called out. They both looked up to see the hotel's concierge, Julian, in his branded gym gear. He entered through the doorway, limbering up, like an Olympian taking to the stage.

Frida groaned and turned to Nesta. "Here we go. Mr Competitive is here."

"Competitive, you say?" asked Nesta. "I never would have guessed."

"He's always trying to challenge me to something. Usually his favourite workouts. As soon as he found out about my weightlifting background, he hasn't left me alone since."

Julian jumped out of his lunge and called out: "Are you talking to me?"

"We're talking *about* you," said Frida, "not *to* you."

"Don't blame you," said Julian, flexing his muscles. "A lot of people in this hotel like to talk about me."

The two women on the stationary bikes ignored his amused snigger and tried to continue with their private conversation.

"I felt terribly sorry for your chef friend," Nesta said. "He seemed very upset about the peanut powder incident with Debbie Backes."

Frida nodded. "That turned out to be the least of her worries. But, yes — Billy has always been a perfectionist. That mistake would have driven him mad."

"Mistake?" asked Julian, who was now pounding away on the exercise bike beside them. "I reckon that guy's the dodgiest chef I've ever seen. Jack the pot washer reckons he's a drug smuggler."

Frida glared at him. "You know that's my friend you're talking about?"

"Come on," said Julian. "You of all people should know he's got his fingers in more pies than that kitchen."

Nesta turned to see that his words were making the receptionist very uncomfortable. "I hear you're something of a challenge beast," she said.

Julian's face lit up. "Sounds like my reputation precedes me. I thought it was just my colleagues who knew about my physical gifts."

"As it happens," Nesta continued, "I'm something of a gym rat myself."

The concierge tried not to laugh. "Really? A gym rat?"

"Oh, yes. They call me Iron Woman back in Bala."

This time, Julian allowed his laugh to escape. "Whatever you say."

"How about we make this next workout interesting." Nesta pointed over to the running machine that almost broke her legs. "You think you can do ten minutes on *Beast Mode*?"

Julian scoffed. "Can *you*?"

"I just did my ten minutes before you walked in. But I'm happy to do it again. That's only if you think you can handle it."

The young man leapt up from his bike and strutted over to the running machine. "I think you might regret this. This isn't my first rodeo. How about I go first?"

Nesta smiled. "You're such a gentleman."

Julian fired up the treadmill and began running as though it was the most natural movement in the world. He pressed a few buttons to initiate *"Beast Mode"* and remained focused on the clock. "Maybe we should make this interesting. How about ten pounds? That's more than your last tip."

Cheeky sod, Nesta thought. She had presumed that a pound was a perfectly appropriate tipping amount. "How about we just stick with a more valuable commodity — pride?"

Julian howled towards the ceiling. "Whatever you say!"

A few minutes later, Julian was really starting to feel the burn. The two women watched, as the man began to sweat profusely, causing him to stop talking altogether (a huge added benefit to the challenge). By minute eight, he was as pale as the hotel's bedsheets and looked as though he might just drop.

"Are you alright?" asked Frida, eventually. Even she was now feeling sorry for the young man.

"I can't feel my legs!" Julian cried. His arms were flailing in the air, until the timer showed mercy and changed to the number ten. As soon as the treadmill ground to a halt, he dropped to his knees and began gasping for air. "Your turn!" he cried, coughing and splurting.

Nesta smiled from the comfort of her stationary bike. "Oh, you know what? Maybe this isn't such a good idea. How about we call the whole thing off? I think I'm going to pass on this one."

Julian began stuttering his way to a response. "But — you

can't just —" Before he could respond, the man dived forward and began vomiting into the nearest waste bin.

His audience of two cringed and watched the weary concierge drag himself out of the gym.

"Wow," said Frida. "Now that was cold. Remind me never to mess with you."

Nesta turned to her with a sigh. "Now that we can continue our conversation in private again," she said, "tell me more about this chef friend of yours."

Frida's smile faded. They continued their cycle, until she could find the best way to answer the question. "Billy's a good guy, really. He just makes stupid mistakes."

"Like getting into bar fights?" asked Nesta.

"You heard about that?" Frida slowed her pace.

"My friend saw the repercussions. He apparently made a right mess of his white uniform."

Frida chuckled. "He's always been more of a lover than a fighter. But he can really wind up the wrong person sometimes."

"Is it true what the pot washer said?"

"Is Billy a drug dealer?" Frida laughed. "He's had his brushes with the law but never drugs. I'm sure he's *consumed* his fair share, though. A lot of chefs do. It's a high-pressure job. They have to unwind somehow."

Nesta began to feel her body get heavy and had forgotten that she was still on an exercise bike. "What kind of brushes did Billy have with the law?"

Frida did a quick scan of the gym. Fortunately, there was only one other person in the room, and he was wearing a pair of headphones. "We're talking theft."

"*Theft?*"

The receptionist was almost embarrassed to even say the word. "This was a very long time ago. Billy would never do anything like that now. He had a tough upbringing and committed a few robberies that landed him with jail time and a criminal record. It was actually in prison that he discovered his love of cooking."

"I assume it wasn't the prison food that inspired him," said Nesta. "I hear that is pretty awful."

"The prison had schemes that offered training for different skills." Frida smiled. "Billy started one of the cooking courses and became obsessed. He started getting shifts in the prison canteen, helping with the food. You'd get all kinds of privileges doing jobs like that in the prison. Funnily enough, it was serving that horrible food that *did* inspire his ambition to become a chef. He told me that it made him want to spend the rest of his life preparing the best meals in the world."

Nesta nodded. "I wonder if some of my school canteen staff felt the same way. If bad food inspires great chefs, those dinner ladies would give Nigela Lawson a run for her money."

The British cultural reference went straight over the Swedish woman's head, and she continued with her tale of rehabilitation and hope. "When Billy was released, he managed to get a job washing dishes in a small hotel. Luckily, they don't tend to do criminal record checks in those kinds of jobs, and he managed to work his way up the ranks."

"Good for him," said Nesta, who had long stopped cycling but was engrossed in her friend's story. "Sounds like a happy ending."

Frida lowered her head with a glimmer of sadness. "Sort of. Unfortunately, the end of his time at our last hotel was not very happy at all." She stopped cycling herself and rested her muscular forearms against the handlebars. "There had been reports of stealing going on in the hotel. Our guests were reporting something every week. That's when the hotel management discovered Billy's record. It made him a prime suspect for all the thefts going on. We're not talking small ones, either. Guests were getting high-value items stolen — like jewellery."

Nesta was genuinely shocked. She had always assumed that her belongings were perfectly safe in a hotel room. "Do you really think he did it?"

Frida shook her head. "I think he was used as a scapegoat. He seemed like the most logical suspect once they found out his background. Either way, Billy lost his job, and he was devastated."

"So you offered him another chance?" Nesta asked. She watched the woman nod.

"I knew his CV would get him the job. It's hard to find a good chef, and the managers were in a hurry." She felt a hand on her shoulder and turned to see Nesta smiling at her.

"You sound like a good friend."

They both continued their leisurely cycle to the sound of the latest dance anthem. It was certainly not Nesta's cup of tea, but she suspected that the fast tempo was better than exercising to Glen Campbell.

After a few more imaginary miles, Nesta turned her mind back to Debbie Backes. "You know," she said, "I was asking Malcolm, the doorman, about the guests he sees coming and going. You probably come into contact with them all, too."

Frida nodded. "Everyone has to check in and check out."

"Exactly," said Nesta. "Have you noticed anyone suspicious over the last couple of weeks? Someone who could have been capable of killing Debbie Backes?"

"Wow," said Frida. "What a question."

"Uh, yes." Nesta blushed. "I have a tendency to ask those."

The receptionist gave it some thought. "Am I looking out for a tall, dark stranger with a sinister face and trenchcoat? Because we get a few of those at this hotel."

Nesta chuckled. "If only it was that easy to spot a murderer." She sighed. "Never mind. It was worth a try."

Frida stopped cycling for a moment and was struck by a sudden thought. "You know, there was this one guest that bothered me."

Nesta also stopped cycling now. "Go on."

"She was a makeup artist," said Frida. "She was a strange woman, anyway. I thought it was odd that a makeup artist didn't wear makeup herself — like an overweight personal trainer."

"Or a skinny chef?" asked Nesta.

The receptionist nodded. "But it was more the fact that she decided to check-out of the hotel the day before Debbie Backes was found dead. Like she knew her services would no longer be needed. She was the only member of the crew to leave the hotel."

"That is strange," said Nesta. "Very strange."

Once these two unlikely training partners had finished their cycle, they headed to the water cooler for some much needed re-hydration.

"So what exactly do you normally do after a workout session?" asked Nesta, who could barely now feel her legs.

Frida had barely broken a sweat and shrugged. "I usually grab a protein shake. Or a recovery bar. Anything substantial enough to replenish the muscles."

Nesta nodded as though she understood perfectly. With a large gulp of her water, she made her own suggestion for some post-workout nourishment. "What about cake?"

CHAPTER 19

Darren stretched out his body against the king-sized feather duvet and let out a deep, satisfied breath. This was the life, he thought. With his favourite comic in hand, all that was missing now was a can of *Coke* and a pizza (things he had contemplated ringing the front desk about). Surely *those* items were on the menu.

As he settled into the next page of his graphic novel, the room's peace and tranquility was shattered by a series of muffled shouting. His concentration broken, Darren let out a grunt and went marching across the hotel room with determined strides.

Over in the hallway, on the other side of the wall, hotel porter Henry was being berated by a furious man in business clothes. "How could you be so stupid?! That thing cost me a bomb — and now I can't even wheel it down the street anymore!"

The guest pointed to the broken wheel on his giant suitcase.

Henry stared at it like a helpless mouse. "Sorry... it came off when I pulled it up the stairs..."

"Then you should have taken better care! You must have really bashed it to death to get a whole wheel off. You might as well have run it over with a van! Now I want to know what you're going to do about it?"

"Hey!" a voice cried out from behind them. "Some people are trying to relax!"

Darren was now standing in the open doorway with a scowl.

"Do you mind?" asked the businessman. "We're trying to have a conversation."

"I thought conversations were supposed to involve *two* people? All I can hear is one loud mouth, blabbering away!"

Henry's jaw dropped open, and he wanted to hide behind the enormous suitcase.

"I beg your pardon?" asked the businessman.

"Why are you picking on that guy, anyway?" Darren pointed at the stunned porter, who was like a small deer facing a pair of very large headlights.

"He's ruined my luggage!" the guest cried.

Darren inspected the suitcase again and folded his arms. "Looks pretty cheap to me. Maybe next time you should carry it yourself. Or get a better one. You get what you pay for."

The furious man didn't know which way to turn. He wasn't going to get sympathy from either person and began pacing around. "This is unbelievable! I'm not going to stand here and take this abuse!"

"What," said Darren, "but the hotel staff can?" He pointed again at Henry. "That guy might not be able to tell you where to go, but I sure can. What are you going to do? Write me a complaint letter?"

The porter wanted the suitcase beside them to swallow him up whole. He watched, as his disgruntled guest huffed one last time before storming off to his room.

"Yeah, that's right!" Darren called after him. "Sod off, you lazy git!"

Once the businessman had disappeared, the teenager turned to see that Henry was staring at him in disbelief.

"Are they all like that?" asked Darren.

The porter didn't even have to think. "Yeah, pretty much. But it's worse when the lift's broken. I had to drag his suitcase up three flights of stairs. No wonder it's knackered."

Darren nodded. "I don't know how you do it. I'm never working in a job that deals with customers. I don't have the patience."

Henry chuckled. "I can already see that. Thanks for your help."

"I just wanted to read my *Watchmen* comic in peace."

"You like Alan Moore?" asked Henry with a twinkle in his eye.

"Course," said Darren. "Who doesn't?"

"I'm more of a *Marvel* fan."

Darren nodded. "Fair play. I can respect that."

The porter was about to walk away, when he was reminded of the broken elevator and paused. "Any chance you could help me carry something upstairs?"

Henry had failed to mention that the object he needed help carrying was the weight of both them. Darren spent the next five minutes groaning his way back up to the fourth floor, as he and the porter lugged up the largest suitcase known to man. The teenager had never felt so much sweat pour from his face and began to worry if he had a serious medical issue.

"Just pop her down there," said Henry, once they had reached the end of the hallway. "Appreciate that."

Darren was still trying to recover. "I think you might have broken my back."

The porter chuckled, until he realised that the teenager was being serious. "Try stretching it off," he said. He went on to pull out two *Mars* bars from his pocket. "Want one of these?"

Darren looked up and accepted the offer with the response of a man having been found wandering through a hot desert. They both took a seat with their backs up against the suitcase and began devouring their chocolate bars.

"Like I said," said Darren. "Don't know how you do it."

"You've never had a part-time job or something?" asked Henry.

"Nope." Darren gave it some more thought. "Actually, I did do a few days at a market stall in Mold once. But that's about it."

Henry shook his head. "That's crazy. I was dying to start working as soon as I was old enough to get a part-time job. But I hate working here."

Darren swallowed a mouthful of chocolate. "Don't blame you. So, why did you want to work so much?"

"I just wanted to start earning money," said Henry. "I realised early on that it was the key to getting what you want. I'll never forget that first payslip. But now I'm not so sure. The way I'm going, I'll end up like my uncle. He's worked at this hotel all his life."

"That's a long time," said Darren. "Especially standing outside of a door."

"You're telling me," said Henry. "I'd much rather be one of the guests. Waiting on people hand and foot gets old real quick."

Darren thought about the king-sized bed waiting for him. "I'm not gonna lie — I kind of like being a guest, too."

"What's your secret?" asked Henry with a smile.

"Secret? To land a few night's stay at this hotel?" Darren had to think about it. "It's a long story. First you have to befriend a retired woman and help her solve mysteries." He saw the confused porter staring at him. "Like I said, it's a long story."

Henry gazed down the hallway at the row of closed doors. The silence of an empty corridor had always disturbed him, and he shuddered. "Well, there's plenty of mysteries in this place.

This old building always gives me the creeps. But I never thought someone could get *killed*."

Darren nodded. "If there's one thing I've learnt this year, it's that there's a killer around every corner."

The teenager's words did nothing to calm the porter's already existing anxiety. "It hasn't felt safe around here since that woman was found dead. I feel like I'm going to walk into another room and find a dead body."

"Imagine the girl who found her," said Darren.

Henry nodded. "That was Amy. I heard she was beside herself. They better catch whoever did this soon. Or I'm handing in my notice."

"They got a few witnesses." Darren didn't seem to have any problems discussing a murder investigation whilst munching on a chocolate bar and continued talking with his mouthful. "One person even saw a woman running out of the victim's room just before they found the body."

A surprised Henry turned to him. "What did this woman look like?"

Darren shook his head. "She didn't see her face, but she went running out of there like a rat from a sinking ship. Like proper sprinting."

"I think I might have seen this person as well," said Henry.

The teenager swallowed his mouthful of chocolate and paused. "When?"

Henry tried to think back. "It was not long before the police were called, and I heard all the commotion. I was at the end of my shift and taking some rubbish out to the bins." He frowned. "That's not actually my job, but the manager asked me to take out a load of cardboard. I was coming back inside through the fire escape, and a woman came running down the staircase. She pushed me out the way and almost knocked me over. I tried to call after her, but she went straight through the open door and out into the street."

Darren had been listening intently. "Did you see her face?"

The porter nodded. "Only briefly. She wasn't wearing makeup or anything, but I could tell she was a woman. She looked really panicky. Like she'd stolen something."

"Or murdered someone?"

Henry gulped. He didn't quite know how to answer that question. "It was weird behaviour. I was going to tell someone, but when I came back to the lobby there was all this commotion about an incident in one of the rooms, and the emergency services were called. I haven't really thought about that woman again until now."

There was another long pause of silence, and Darren polished off the rest of his *Mars* bar before climbing to his feet. He reached out his hand and helped the porter up. "Any chance you can show me where this all happened?"

CHAPTER 20

Nesta wrapped a towel around her swimming costume and headed in search of the sauna. Despite her initial plan for a quick dip in the hotel pool, she had been advised by Frida that a highly-effective method of recovery after a good workout was, in fact, a sauna. The thought of sitting in a boiling hot shack was hardly Nesta's first choice of place to relax, but, with her aching leg muscles and fast approaching build-up of lactic acid, she was willing to try anything.

"Shack" had been the perfect word to describe this sauna, which resembled a place where she normally stored her gardening tools (not that they came out very often). Nesta opened up the door and was struck in the face by a burst of heat. Perhaps this was a bad idea after all, and she was about to turn the other way, when she heard a voice from inside.

"It's alright. There's plenty of room."

Nesta reluctantly entered her new torture chamber with an even stiffer body than before and didn't want to appear prudish. The man sitting in his swimming costume was Gary, the prop master. His bald head was already bright red, and his face was dripping with sweat.

His new companion sat herself down against the wooden bench and prepared to endure the heat. "It's not the most pleasant environment, is it?" she muttered.

"I really like it," said Gary. "There's something about sweating everything out that gives me pleasure. I enjoy a bit of suffering."

Nesta was beginning to think that she was hanging out with a raving lunatic and had a right mind to run for her life. "I've already done my fair share of suffering for one day. My legs are killing me."

"This should help," said Gary. "What you want to do afterwards is jump straight into an ice bath."

Nesta let out a nervous cry of laughter. "That's a good one! What psychopath would do something like that?"

Gary stared at her with a serious expression. "I try and do it most days."

"Oh," said Nesta. "You have an ice bath in your house?"

The man smiled and shook his head. "You can spend a fortune ordering ice baths online. But I made my own one. You just need to get an empty wheelie bin, right? Cut the lid off, then store a load of ice cubes in your freezer. When you're ready for a dip, you fill up the bin with your garden hose and add the ice. Works brilliantly!"

Now it was Nesta's turn to stare. "And you do this regularly at this time of year?"

"I do it all year round," said Gary. "It makes you feel fantastic! Trust me, you should try it."

"Even in the winter?"

"*Especially* in winter."

Nesta let out another nervous laugh. Her wheelie bin was strictly for rubbish, and she had no intention of replacing it with herself. "You must be a glutton for punishment."

Gary nodded. "I've always had quite a high pain threshold.

My mother used to say that. Probably just as well on this film shoot!" He let out a loud cackle. "Hey! Did you want to stick some more water on that thing?"

The man pointed towards the metal basket in the corner of the room. It was filled with dark coals that glowed faintly, providing the source of this immense heat. Beside Nesta was a bucket of water with a wooden ladle. She put two and two together and was more than happy to pour cold water across this burning furnace if that's what the man wanted.

"Just a little bit," Gary warned.

Nesta ignored him and poured a generous amount of water from the bucket itself. That should cool it down a bit, she thought. To her great surprise, the enormous hiss from the burning coals was followed by a cloud of steam, along with a rolling wave of intense heat that prickled her skin. "Oh!" she cried.

Gary howled with laughter. "You really *do* like it hot!"

Nesta desperately wanted to run for the door but was determined not to give this cocky man the satisfaction and forced herself back down on the bench.

"Wow," said Gary, wiping his wet face. "You're pretty hardcore."

Nesta went silent for a moment and felt as though she was sitting next to Satan himself in the fires of hell. "It's no big deal."

They listened to the sizzling water for a few minutes, until Gary opened his mouth again. He couldn't stand a long silence and felt obliged to fill one at any given opportunity. "You know that I always secretly knew who took that hand?"

Nesta turned to look at him. "Hand? You mean, the severed one?"

Gary sniggered. "How many hands have you come across recently?" His amusement was not reciprocated, and he could tell the woman was weary of him. He had never been very well-liked but had never quite understood why. He usually kept to himself and his love of prop-making. When not on set, the job of a prop master was a fairly lonely one. "The person who took it didn't even know I was watching him."

"*Him*?" asked Nesta.

The man grinned. "Ah, so you *are* interested." Gary folded up his arms and enjoyed holding in his little secret. "It's someone from this hotel, actually. Luckily for him, it was an old prop from a film I did years ago. Never needed it again, but you never know. I assumed the guy was a prop enthusiast like my younger self. My dad used to work as a maintenance man at *Pinewood Studios*. He'd often let me wander the place as he worked, and I saw all kinds of classics being shot. The *Carry On* films were my favourites, and I saw loads of them being shot. They looked a right laugh."

Nesta would have taken an interest had she not been struggling with the heat and couldn't bring herself to say anything.

"But it was the sets themselves that really appealed to me," Gary continued. "I often would sneak a few keepsakes in my bag to take home when nobody was looking. My most prized possession was a pistol from *Moonraker* — not Roger Moore's, sadly. It belonged to one of the henchmen." He experienced a surge of nostalgia at the thought of his youth (although it could have been just the high temperature). "So, when I found this person poking around in my prop truck, I saw a glimmer of myself. I just let the guy take it. You can imagine my surprise when it turned up on Debbie Backes' pillow. Turned out that it was all just some big prank. But at least I got my hand back."

"You don't think there was any connection between this so-called prank and the murder?" Nesta asked.

Gary was surprised to hear her voice. She looked a little woozy. "Who knows? After all, my hand wasn't the only thing stolen recently."

His words gave Nesta another burst of energy, and she lifted up her head. "Go on. And make it quick! I'm not going to last in here much longer."

"Well, according to one of the makeup artists — who heard it from the hotel manager —" Gary lowered his voice. "Apparently, the guy's one of those annoying autograph hunters. He's been after one from Bella Marsh ever since she started and has been trying to get one through any crew member he can find. Anyway, the manager told Jessica that they discovered Debbie's necklace was stolen on the day of her murder."

Nesta could still picture that hypnotic diamond around Debbie's neck. She hadn't remembered seeing it, however, when Debbie was lying on her hotel room floor. "Whoever killed her must have taken the necklace."

"Bingo," said Gary. "And it's worth a few bob, too. I looked it up. That person now has more money than this film budget."

Nesta felt her head begin to throb, and she tried to stand up.

"Calling it a day already?" asked Gary with a snort.

"It depends," said Nesta, heading over to the sizzling rocks and lifting up another full bucket of water. The sight of her daring expression wiped the smile from Gary's face, and he looked down, nervously, at the bucket. "How about you tell me exactly who planted that severed hand on Debbie's pillow? Unless you fancy another round?"

CHAPTER 21

Nesta peered up the flight of concrete stairs and turned around. "Are you really filming this?"

Darren continued to hold up his phone with a thumbs-up.

"It's just a load of steps," said Nesta, whilst opening up the fire escape doors. "We're hardly in Georgetown looking up those stairs from *The Excorcist*."

"Don't you mean the *Rocky* steps?" asked Darren. "I'd say they're probably more recognisable."

Nesta hadn't realised until now how many famous staircases there were in film history but didn't have time to deliberate any further at that moment. "So this was definitely where the young man saw her?"

Darren nodded and pointed to the open door. "She ran straight out through there."

"And what was she wearing?"

"The porter said she had a striped, black and yellow dress — and a bright-green cardigan over her shoulders."

Nesta's eyes widened. "Did she have red, curly hair?"

The teenager nodded and watched her disappear through

the doorway. Outside, there was a large commercial wheelie bin in a narrow side street.

Nesta began searching behind it but came out with her hands empty.

"What are you looking for?" asked Darren.

"What you've just described," Nesta said, "is the exact costume and hair of Appie from *Steeping Road*."

"The soap opera?" Darren shuddered at the mere thought of what he would describe as the tackiest show on television. "Surely the character wears lots of outfits. What makes you think one of them is *that* one?"

Nesta rolled her eyes at his gap in soap opera knowledge. "Firstly, nobody wears a bright-green cardigan over a dress that looks like a bumble bee. And, secondly, the whole joke is that Appie is always wearing the same thing. It's like her signature outfit. Like Noddy with his red top and blue hat. You don't see *him* rocking up one day in a black t-shirt and a beanie."

Darren began scratching his head. "So you're saying that the porter bumped into a fictional character?"

"Of course not," Nesta snapped. "This person was obviously dressed as Appie Finn. Debbie had the costume in her room — including the wig!"

"Wig?" asked Darren.

"Appie Finn had red, curly hair. Debbie was a natural blonde, so she always had to wear a wig every time." Nesta paused. "I suppose it's a bit like casting an American to play an English part. Filmmakers seem to like to make life harder for themselves — *and* their actors." She looked back at the wheelie bin. "What do you reckon?"

Darren could read her mind and began holding up his hands in protest. "No! Absolutely not! There's no chance I'm getting in that thing."

Moments later, and the teenager was fully submerged in

rubbish, with only the top of his head poking out of the open dumpster.

"Found anything yet?" Nesta called out. She had been given the privilege of recording the moment on Darren's phone and held up the device so that she could make sure she was capturing everything. This was certainly something that she could imagine watching back in the future (if not only for her own amusement).

"It stinks in here!" Darren cried back. His groaning and whining soon stopped, when he stumbled on a screwed-up ball of material. He lifted up a red wig and a dress that used to be black and yellow. Now it was covered in a substance that Darren didn't even want to *try* and identify.

"Haha!" Nesta cried, clapping her hands. "I was right. You see! That was well worth climbing into the bin for."

"You wouldn't be saying that if you saw what else is in here," said Darren, dragging himself back out again. "Besides, I don't really see how this helps us much. So someone decided to dress up in Debbie's costume. So what?"

"It *means*," Nesta snapped, "that the person fleeing the scene of the crime could still be anyone — male or female!"

"So we're back to square one again? Great!"

Nesta pointed towards a discarded carrier bag beside the wheelie bin. "Stick the wig and clothes in there. This could end up being a valuable piece of evidence. Try not to touch it too much."

Darren dangled the stained dress with the tips of his fingers. "You think I want to touch this smelly thing?"

They both headed back inside the building with plenty of food for thought. Nesta had shared the identity of the severed hand prankster, and it had only left the teenager even more confused.

"The waiter?" Darren asked, as they entered the hotel lobby. "The one with the beard? Why would *he* want to kill Debbie?"

"It doesn't mean he actually *killed* her," said Nesta. "But he also probably served her the meal. So he could have also planted the peanut powder. The question we need to ask is — why would he do that?"

"He wouldn't have much time to pour peanut powder on the mash. Someone would have seen him."

"Depends on how skilled he was." Nesta pressed the call button for the lift and was relieved to see that it was working again (her tired legs couldn't handle any more stairs). They entered the lift, and she gave Darren an excited smile. "I could ask him about it tonight on my dinner date."

Darren rolled his eyes. "You really don't switch off. No wonder you don't like retirement."

"On the contrary," said Nesta. "Retirement has been the best thing that's ever happened to me. I'm having a great time."

The lift doors opened again, and they both stepped out onto the fourth floor.

"So who am I supposed to have dinner with?" Darren asked, as they entered the hotel room. "I'm not sitting on my own like Billy-no-mates."

Nesta could sense that he was sulking and started to feel a little guilty. "How about your new porter friend?"

Darren scoffed. "I'm not asking some guy I bumped into for five minutes out to dinner. Do you know how sad that is? I'm not *that* desperate. I'll just get a takeaway and eat it in the room."

"Suit yourself," said Nesta. She headed over to her suitcase in search of something to wear and had a sudden thought. "How did he get in the room?"

Darren was already in his favourite spot, lounging on the bed. He looked around and gave her a confused frown. "How did *who* get in the room?"

Nesta lifted up her room key card. "The waiter. Both he and the killer needed to get into Debbie's room without her noticing. Now, she may have invited the killer into the room, if she knew who they were. But not the waiter. *He* had to sneak in to plant the severed hand. How did he get into the room?"

"He must have had a spare key card," said Darren.

"Exactly," said Nesta. "But a waiter from the dining hall doesn't have access to those. So how did he get one?"

Darren didn't have the answer to her question, but both of them were certain of one thing — there was something very strange going on in that hotel.

CHAPTER 22

Nesta and Malcolm sat opposite each other, hiding behind their menus. They had barely said a word since arriving at their table and were both dying to remedy the situation.

Nesta had just realised that this was the first so-called "date" she had been on since losing her husband, and, all of a sudden, it was like being an insecure teenager again. In actual fact, she had not really *dated* anyone even before meeting Morgan. Most of the relationships she had known in Bala tended to happen more organically rather than off the back of a trip to the cinema or a meal. Everyone in *her* youth already knew each other anyway, and romantic relationships were often formed down the local pub or during a trip to *The Royal Welsh Show*.

"Is there anything that you would recommend?" Nesta asked.

Malcolm, who already looked lost in the depths of his overwhelming menu, shrugged. "I couldn't say. I've never actually eaten here."

Nesta dropped down her laminated piece of card. "Are you

serious? You've worked at this hotel most of your life and never actually eaten here?"

The doorman shook his head. "Oh, no. It's far too expensive. I much prefer to bring a sandwich to work."

The woman opposite him burst out laughing. "We didn't have to eat here, you know? I'm also quite partial to a sandwich."

Malcolm's cheeks went red, and he nodded. "Yes, maybe this was a silly choice."

"I don't normally eat oysters and steak tartare," said Nesta. "I might seem like I have a stick up my backside, but I'm actually only staying here on a questionably-sourced gift certificate."

"Oh, no. I never assumed you had a stick up your —" Malcolm saw her raised eyebrow and coughed. "We can go somewhere else, if you like?"

Nesta shook her head. "This place will do just fine. It's the company that counts."

The doorman blushed again. "Well, then. I think a bottle of red is in order?"

"Absolutely," said Nesta. She saw their waiter approaching, and her face lit up. "Ah, garçon!"

Leigh arrived with his usual polite smile, something he had perfected over years of public interaction without being in the mood. "Can I get you something to drink?"

"Why, yes." Nesta gave him a mischievous smirk. "You could certainly give us a *hand*." She waited for a reaction, but the man's professional demeanour was as solid as a rock. "In fact, *props* to you for coming over so quickly." Still nothing.

"Can we get a bottle of your finest red wine, please?" asked Malcolm.

"I'll see what I can do," said Leigh.

Nesta waited for the waiter to disappear. "Malcolm! You're really pushing the boat out."

"Well, you have to live a little." He looked down at his cutlery, and a slight sadness washed over him. "I've probably spent more of my life earning a living than actually making the time to spend any of the money. A bit late to realise that, I know."

"Not at all," said Nesta. "You're not alone in that regard. I think most people have to wait until our age before they learn what's important. I bet if you went back in time to tell your younger self to work less, he wouldn't listen anyway."

Malcolm chuckled. "No, he probably wouldn't. Stubborn sod."

There was another silence, only, this time, it was more comfortable. Malcolm looked around at the dining hall he had spent so little time in. Many of his work colleagues had spotted him straight away and were taking curious glances in his direction, as well as his female dinner date. "I never imagined I would think about retirement," he said. "But I'm thinking my time has finally come to step aside. You know it's the right decision when most of the other staff are half your age."

"You'll have big shoes to fill," said Nesta.

"Well, I *am* a size fifteen." Malcolm chuckled. "I was rather hoping for Henry to take over once he'd earnt his stripes."

"You don't think he will?"

The doorman sighed. "I can tell his heart isn't really in it. He's just doing it to please me, which is not a sustainable reason."

"What was your reason?" asked Nesta.

"My father was a plumber," Malcolm said with a fond smile. "He used to work all the hours he could. Proper grafter. One time he got this job at one of the posh hotels to fix a toilet. I waited in his van across the street. Once he'd finished the job, we both had cheese sandwiches and watched the people going in and out of the hotel. He told me that he'd take me to stay in a hotel like that one day. He spent about half an hour describing what he had seen inside the building: the lobby, the room, the big hallways... then, I turned my attention to the doorman. The man was so smart in his big coat and top hat. He had such a presence and commanded respect from every guest that went past. My dad joked about how *that* person would never be found bending over a toilet bowl with his hands dirty. I never forgot that moment of watching the hotel doorman at work."

Nesta could see him basking in the happy memory. "You must have been so thrilled the day you got the job."

Malcolm chuckled. "I couldn't believe my luck. I'd started my plumbing apprenticeship, and we landed a job at *The Legion*. We were there for a few days, and I found out that there was an opening for a porter. It was a big risk, but I gave up my apprenticeship and went for the job. I'd built up a good rapport with the hotel manager at the time, and he gave me the job. I figured that being a porter was the closest thing to the role I really wanted, and the doorman at the time was on the verge of retirement. The rest was history."

"Your father must have been so proud," said Nesta.

The doorman's smile vanished. "Not exactly. Sadly, my father hadn't quite shared the same admiration for the doorman that day in the van. He found the role a bit of a joke and considered plumbing to be a far more respectable profession. My father was crushed when he heard I'd given up my apprenticeship to take the hotel job. He said I was a fool. But it was too late by then. I'd made the choice and had to stick with it. I think that's why I always took the job so seriously and worked all the hours I could. I was terrified of having made the wrong call and my father saying that he'd told me so."

"I'm sorry to hear that," said Nesta, who hadn't expected such a sad end to the man's story.

"Still," said Malcolm, lifting up his chin. "I'd say I'd made the right call in the end. I've had a long career. Even my father couldn't argue with that. God rest his soul." He looked up to see her staring at him. "That's more than enough about me. How about you? Tell me about your life."

Nesta was caught off guard. She had always been more interested in other people's stories and hated discussing herself. "Oh, well. I was an English secondary school teacher for most of my life. I had two children. Both have now long flown the nest and left me with my Jack Russell, Hari. My husband, Morgan, is sadly no longer with us of course. And I live in the town of Bala."

Malcolm chuckled. "I wasn't asking for a biography. I want to know about *you*. What you like — what you don't like! Who is Nesta *today*? Not who she was *yesterday*."

Nesta thought his questions were quite rich coming from a man who had just divulged his own past but decided to humour him. What she wasn't going to disclose was her newfound interest in solving crimes. Nobody was ready for that on a first date, and she didn't want to scare him away.

Her response was saved by the appearance of Leigh with their bottle of wine, and she waited for him to pour her a sample.

"Are we sure it's safe?" Nesta asked, lifting the glass up to her lips with a snort of laughter. The two men either side of her weren't nearly as amused, and she took what she hoped wasn't her last gulp. "Mmmmh. That's lovely!"

Leigh poured them both a drink, and they both *clinked* their glasses.

"To new friends," said Malcolm.

"To new friends."

They ordered their meals, and the waiter disappeared before Nesta could get a chance to ask him a question. She saw him heading to the other side of the dining hall, where he began chatting with another member of staff.

Malcolm was just about to open his mouth, when she stood up suddenly. "Would you excuse me a moment? I really wanted to ask that waiter about the origin of this lovely wine. I won't be a tick."

"Oh," said Malcolm, a little perplexed. "By all means."

Nesta scurried off across the dining hall, leaving the man to enjoy the rest of his glass alone.

"There you are," said Nesta, cornering the waiter once his colleague had walked away. "I've been meaning to speak with you."

A confused Leigh tried to remain professional. "Is there a problem with the wine?"

"The wine is perfect." She looked around before lowering her voice. "I'm just worried about my mashed potato."

Leigh's eyes widened. "Excuse me?"

"I think you know what I'm talking about," Nesta said, locking in a hard stare. "You seem to be quite the prankster. I wouldn't like to be the next unfortunate victim."

The waiter began to stutter. "I — that's — what exactly are you implying?"

"I'm saying that *you're* the one who put that severed hand on Debbie Backes' pillow. You were caught red-handed when you stole it from the props van." Nesta paused to re-consider her use of the words "red-handed" but shook it off. "Anyway, my question to you is — why? Was it just for a laugh? Were you trying to scare her? Or get her back for something?"

Leigh's face went pink, and he had to loosen his collar. "Do we have to discuss this here? I'm supposed to be working."

"Did you also spike Debbie's mash with the peanut powder?"

"What?!" The waiter's eyes kept darting from side to side to make sure that no one was listening. "No! The peanut powder was definitely not me. On my mother's life! Careful what you say — or people will go around saying it's true."

"You went to the trouble of frightening her with a prosthetic hand. It wouldn't take that much more effort to spike her food."

"That was completely different!" Leigh realised that he was raising his voice and paused to take a breath. "Listen, yes, I stuck a harmless prop in her room. But that's as far as I would ever go. I would never mess with a person's food, especially one with a serious allergy."

Nesta studied his face. She had spoken to enough liars to sense that he might be telling the truth. But you could never be certain. "If it wasn't you who spiked the mash, then who was it? Because a person who is capable of messing with a peanut allergy is probably capable of something a lot more serious..." He knew exactly what she was implying *this* time, Nesta thought, and hoped that it was enough to get her answers.

A flustered Leigh looked out across the busy dining hall. Guests were laughing and chatting amongst themselves, and he scanned the entire room until his eyes landed on a single person. "It was her."

Nesta could see his gaze following a young waitress making her way back to the kitchen. "Are you sure? *She* spiked Debbie's mash?"

Leigh nodded. "Yes. It was Amy."

CHAPTER 23

When Nesta finally returned to her table, she sat down with a distant expression.

"Is everything alright?" asked Malcolm. He had watched her conversation with Leigh go on for quite some time, and, judging by her confused face, he was genuinely concerned.

"Hmh?" Nesta asked.

"The red wine. You wanted to find out more about it?"

"Oh! Yes!" Nesta snapped out of her trail of thought and returned to the present moment. "I'm sorry. It turned out that the wine had quite a long history. It's a rare grape variety, you see."

Malcolm picked up the bottle and squinted at the bottle. "A Merlot?"

"Ah, look! Our food is arriving." She clapped her hands, as Amy approached her table with a plate in each hand.

Nesta studied her every move like a wide-eyed cat on the other side of a bird cage.

"Can I get you anything else?" Amy asked after the diners had been served their food.

"All good here," said Malcolm, smiling and rubbing his hands. He had not eaten a Beef Wellington since he was a lad.

"Same." Nesta waited for her to walk away and covered her mouth. "Oh, heavens. I forgot to ask her for the mustard." She disappeared again, leaving Malcolm very confused. He leant across the table and studied her meal.

"Mustard with fish?"

Amy was heading back to the kitchen, only, this time, Nesta was in hot pursuit.

"Amy! Amy, wait!"

The waitress froze just outside the kitchen door and turned around.

"How are you?" Nesta asked, running over.

Amy slowly recognised her and nodded. "Uh, I'm good. Thanks."

"It's good to see you back at work. Not too soon, I hope?"

"I just wanted to forget about —" She saw a flash of Debbie's body in her mind and shuddered. "You know — *that* whole thing. I figured the quickest way to get back to normal was to carry on working. How about you?"

Nesta placed a hand against her own chest. "It's all too soon for me, still, I'm afraid. But it's good to see that you're still soldiering on." She looked around and saw Leigh serving a table with their drinks. "I was talking to your colleague, actually. Would you say he's a bit of a prankster?"

Amy frowned. "Prankster? No, not really. He's a bit boring, actually. But don't say that I told you that."

"Boring?" Nesta nodded. "How strange. He seemed to have a lot to say about you."

The waitress' frown deepened. "About me? Like *what*?"

"You wouldn't say that you were close?"

"We work together. And we go out for drinks with the same group of friends. Maybe he thinks that we're closer friends than we are. The guy's been working here far too long. He's seen lots of people come and go over the years. I can't imagine he gets that close with *anyone*."

"Are there any work colleagues in this group of friends?" Nesta asked.

"Yeah," said Amy. "They're all work colleagues. We barely get time for a normal social life here, so some of us go out for a drink after work. They call us *The Ten O'Clock Crew*. Because most of us finish at ten. A few other people tag along too."

"You go out every night?"

Amy shook her head. "Only on Thursdays. We all head to *The Last Hour* pub in town which doesn't close until two. If it's Thursday, and it's ten o'clock, you can guarantee you'll find us there. Whether we've been working that day or not. I guess it's sort of a tradition for those in the know."

"And who exactly is in the know?" asked Nesta. "The front-of-house staff?"

"Not just front-of-house," said Amy. "The kitchen staff, hotel staff — anyone who's been invited. There's sort of a circle of trust. So you won't find any management there."

"What about your head chef?"

Amy smiled. "Billy's a bit of an exception. He's been there from the start." She heard a call from inside the kitchen. "I better get back to work. It's busy tonight."

Nesta watched her disappear through the kitchen door and nodded.

By the time she had returned to her table, Malcolm had already poured himself another glass of wine and was waiting in front of an untouched plate of food.

"You should have started without me," said Nesta. "You didn't have to wait."

"I never forget my manners," said Malcolm. His voice was already starting to slur from too much wine on an empty stomach. He had never been much of a drinker. "Besides, the whole purpose is to enjoy our dinner together. Did you get the mustard?"

"Mustard? Oh, yes! The mustard." Nesta pulled a weary face. "They were all out, sadly. Never mind."

They both tucked into their meals and said very little until the plates were empty.

"That was simply divine," said Nesta, patting down her mouth with a napkin. "How was yours?"

A bloated Malcolm scrunched up his face. "If I'm being honest, it was a bit disappointing. The beef was tough and the pastry was a little soggy. But I suppose I can't really complain when I work here!" He let out a laugh and grabbed his menu. "Maybe I'll have better luck with the desserts. You can only go so wrong with them, eh?"

Nesta made a series of humming noises like she had tasted the best meal of her entire life. "You know what? I simply have to give that chef my compliments. It really was delicious." She climbed to her feet.

"You're going *now*?" asked Malcolm.

"Some meals just need to be praised immediately. I'll be right back!"

Malcolm sighed and continued browsing his desert section.

Over in the kitchen, one of the sous chefs was busy plating up an intricate dish as if it were a game of *Buckaroo*. Just as he placed the final piece, he turned to see a woman standing beside him and jumped, causing his masterpiece to crumble.

"Is Billy around?" Nesta asked.

The disgruntled sous chef let out a grunt and pointed towards the back door. "He's having a smoke."

Nesta headed straight outside to a small courtyard. Billy was, as predicted, standing in the corner, blowing smoke out into the cool air.

"There you are," said Nesta.

The head chef could not have been more surprised to see her walking out of his kitchen and almost swallowed his cigarette. "Can I help you?"

"Yes, I think you can." Nesta took a seat on a stack of boxes and crossed her arms. "I may have got to the bottom of who put peanut powder in Debbie's mash. You're right to be distrustful of the waiting staff."

Billy chuckled. "I told you so. Although, it wouldn't have taken a sleuth to work that one out. Not that it matters much now. The woman's dead, anyway. And not because of my food."

Nesta nodded. "I've been getting to you know your Swedish friend this week. She's told me a lot about you."

"She's no friend of mine." He rubbed the bruise on his face. "Would a friend do this?"

"*Frida* did that to you?" Nesta asked with a gasp.

Billy realised that he had over-shared and shrugged his bruise off as though it were merely a scratch. "She doesn't know her own strength sometimes. We were only mucking about. Now what was it you wanted?"

Nesta took her time with the response and watched the steam pouring out of an extractor pipe. "It's very admirable how you've managed to turn your life around. It can't have been easy getting to where you are with a criminal record."

The head chef took another drag of nicotine and stared at her suspiciously. "Frida really has been talking a lot. What else did she say?"

"Only that you went from being a criminal thief to a well-respected chef," said Nesta. "Some might say that it would make a great story for a film."

Billy laughed. "*Me*? She called *me* a thief?" He twirled around and chucked away his cigarette butt. Her comments had clearly touched a nerve, and the man was fuming. "I got in trouble with the law a few times, but that woman was on a whole other level."

"Frida?"

"Oh, yeah. She might seem all nice and innocent. But that woman used to corrupt cleaners and have them steal for her. She used to land jobs at different hotels where she could gain access to hotel rooms. People leave valuables in their rooms all the time, and she took advantage of that."

"How did she keep getting jobs?"

Billy shrugged. "Different names, fake references, fake CVs — the woman's a fraudster. She stole thousands from the last hotel we worked at."

"The one in Paris?"

The man nodded. "But as soon as the hotel starts to investigate internally, she hands in her notice. There's been a few times that she's tried to get me involved in her little schemes, and in Paris I did. But we all got caught. So, Frida fled for the UK and found this hotel."

"She mentioned that it was her who got you the job here," said Nesta.

Billy nodded. "We'd always been good mates. I like the girl and was grateful for the chance to start again. No more stupid games. But I should have known better." His eyes burned with anger. "By the time I got here, she was already up to her old tricks and trying to plan her next score. But I refused to be involved. It was time to grow up."

"Did she have her sights on a certain diamond necklace belonging to a famous actor by any chance?" Nesta asked.

Billy glared at her. "How do you know about that?"

Nesta nodded. "So there *was* a plan."

The head chef was struck by a sudden feeling of panic. "Now, look — it had nothing to do with me, alright? I wanted no part of it!"

"What about *The Ten O'Clock Crew*?"

The courtyard went silent for a moment.

"What was it you wanted from me, exactly?" asked Billy. "I need to get back to work."

Nesta smiled. "I came to offer my compliments on the fish. It was excellent."

The head chef shook his head and disappeared back into the kitchen.

Nesta made the long walk back to her table, and when she got there, her date had seemingly vanished. She looked at the empty chair opposite hers and let out a disappointed sigh. "Oh, Malcolm. I'm sorry..."

CHAPTER 24

Nesta and Darren emerged from *The Legion Hotel* on what was a gloriously sunny morning. They had both experienced very different evenings the night before, and only one of them was interested in sharing.

"So I finished the pizza, watched a bit of *Family Fortunes* and just fell asleep." Darren waited for Nesta to tell him about her dinner date, but she remained tight-lipped.

"Have they told you the name of your character?" the teenager asked, as they headed underneath the Eastgate Clock.

Nesta checked her slip of paper. "It just says *Woman On Street*. But I've been promised a line."

They turned right in the direction of Chester's great cathedral, past the war memorial with its prominent stone monument and through into Abbey Square, an area lined with Georgian townhouses. The usually open space was now taken over by a large film crew with their parked lorries and bright lights.

"It certainly *looks* like we've stepped back in time," said Nesta, gazing around at the historical square.

"You could say the same thing about this whole city," said

Darren, raising up his phone to capture the busy film set. "So, where's your trailer at?"

Nesta gave him a playful nudge, and she caught sight of producer Felix Melvin standing nearby. The nervous man was standing back to observe the busy film crew at work and kept biting away at his nails.

"Felix?" asked Nesta, appearing by his side. The man turned to look at her, and, when he didn't recognise her, turned his nose up and tried to ignore this outgoing stranger. "I'm so sorry about your auntie."

The mere mention of his deceased relative caused Felix's frosty demeanour to thaw slightly. "Yes, well. We all are."

"I was such a fan of hers," said Nesta. "I've watched *Steeping Road* all my life. It won't be the same without her."

"The sooner they catch whoever was responsible, the better." Felix's eyes were hidden behind the reflection in his glasses, but it was easy to detect their anger. "I could just about handle losing her to natural causes. But to lose her at the hands of a murderer... it doesn't bear thinking about."

"I hear she also had her necklace stolen."

Felix turned his stiff head and stared at her properly for the first time. "Where did you hear that?"

"It's pretty well common knowledge by this point. We're not talking about *any* old necklace."

"No," Felix snapped. "It was a precious family heirloom. What my aunt was thinking carrying that thing around on her all day I'll never know."

"I imagine that she would have left it to someone in the family," said Nesta, fully aware that she was crossing a line.

"I would say that's none of your business," said the producer. "Can I ask your name? And do you have permission to be on this set?"

"Nesta!" a voice called from behind them.

Nesta turned around to see American producer Jay Bergman heading over with open arms. "So good to see you again," Jay said with his charming voice. "And I see you've met our beloved British guv'nor!"

Jay patted his fellow producer on the back a little too hard. "Don't look so worried," he said. "We're making movies here! It's supposed to be fun."

Felix maintained his gloomy expression. He had never found joy or pleasure, whatsoever, in his experience working in the film industry and figured it was easy to have fun when you had a blank cheque book like Jay. Making films to him was no different to manufacturing tins of dog food. Business was business (and at least the dog food didn't have creative aspirations).

"Are you ready for your big moment, Nessy?"

Nesta felt a swarm of butterflies invading her stomach. "I think so," she said.

"Think?!" Jay clapped his hands and laughed. "You're an actor now. You have to grab each role by the horns and own it. Believe me, this role is perfect for you."

"Do you know when I can get a copy of the script?"

Jay unleashed his pearly, white teeth. "Trust me, you're not gonna need a script for this part. It's just one line. I'm sure you can handle it."

The producer put an arm around Felix and walked him away.

Nesta turned to Darren in horror. "I don't think I can do this."

"What?" asked the confused teenager. "I thought you were *dying* to make your onscreen debut? You told me you've done musicals."

"That was a local production back in Bala," said Nesta. "This is Hollywood!"

"You'll be fine. Don't let that Bond villain make you

nervous." He lifted up his mobile phone. "Just pretend you're doing one of our crime videos."

Nesta smiled and took a deep breath.

"Are you *Woman On Street*?" asked a hurried voice.

Nesta turned to see a young woman with a headset and clipboard. "Uh, yes. That sounds like me."

"We need you in hair and makeup — ASAP!"

The production assistant ushered Nesta away like a stray sheep and led her to a small tent. Before she knew it, Nesta was sitting in front of a brightly-lit mirror, dressed in a Victorian frock that seemed to fit quite nicely.

All of a sudden, her nerves had vanished, and she was rather enjoying being treated like a professional actor.

"Are you ready for your makeup?" asked Charlotte, a woman with enormous glasses and a tired face.

"Absolutely," said Nesta, sitting back in her chair and feeling like she was down at her local salon. "I actually purposely avoided any makeup this morning, realising that you would probably have something specific in mind. I didn't want to mess anything up. I'm not nearly as skilled as you makeup artists."

"Great," said Charlotte, who proceeded to smother Nesta's entire face with a layer of thick, brown paste. The result was the complexion of someone who hadn't washed in a very long time.

"Are you sure this is the right look?" asked Nesta in a slight state of shock.

"Oh, yes." The makeup artist moved on to the hair and began running her fingers through it with a product that caused a style similar to a crow's nest.

Nesta tried to distract herself from the horror of her own appearance by making conversation. "Is it true that Debbie Backes' hair and makeup artist is no longer with us?"

Charlotte paused her assault of Nesta's hair and looked at her strangely. "You mean Debbie Backes is no longer with us?"

"I heard that her personal makeup person had also left the shoot rather abruptly," said Nesta. "Rita?"

"*Rita*?" asked Charlotte. "There's no Rita on this crew."

Nesta thought back to her conversation with Frida. "That girl really *is* a liar," she thought.

"I wish Debbie *had* brought her own personal makeup artist," said Charlotte. "She was a nightmare. Wouldn't let me do anything with her."

Nesta took another look at her own reflection in the mirror and wasn't all that surprised.

"I've done this job for thirty years," Charlotte continued. "And I've done at least a dozen costume dramas. I'd like to think I know what I'm doing. But that woman seemed to always know best."

"How are you finding Bella?" Nesta asked.

Charlotte rolled her eyes. "That's like asking who's worse — Dick Dastardly or Captain Hook? These veteran actors are all the same. But at least Bella lets me do her hair without complaining."

Nesta emerged from the tent like an old hermit squinting at the sun. Darren caught sight of her and ran over.

"What happened to *you*?" he asked. "Fall down a chimney?"

"Don't you dare get me on camera like this," Nesta warned, as he began waving his phone in her face.

"People in the olden days really had strange makeup."

Nesta was about to take out her frustrations on the teenager's phone, when she was whisked away by the energetic production assistant.

"They need you on set right now," said the young woman with the earpiece.

They marched straight past the stone column in the centre of the enormous courtyard, until they reached one of the many Georgian houses flanking the square.

Phil Wogan, a tall man in a long coat, stood outside a blue front door that was being altered by a pair of set dressers.

"I know you," said Nesta, as she approached. "You're that opera singer!"

Phil stared down his nose at her, having been miffed by the vague recognition. In his own mind, he wasn't just "some opera singer", and, in *his* world, people knew him by name.

"Sorry," he said. "I'm afraid that I'm working right now."

"So am I," said Nesta, raising out her arms in excitement. "I believe we have a scene together."

Phil took another look at this dishevelled-looking woman and frowned. "We *have*?"

"I'm *Woman On Street*!"

The opera singer lifted up his script and checked the page. "Oh, right. I wondered where she was."

"What's a singer like you doing on a film like this?" Nesta asked.

"We opera singers act as well as sing," the large man snapped. "My agent thought this would be a good opportunity to get into films. I'm playing Tankford."

"You are?" Nesta clapped her hands. "He's a right nasty piece of work in the book. Doesn't last long, though. In fact, I think he gets killed off in a couple of chapters."

Phil cringed and tried to hide his frustration. "Yes, I believe he does."

"Oh, well." She patted him on the shoulder. "I wouldn't get too down on yourself. I'm barely in the film, myself. Quality over quantity, eh?"

The man shuddered, and they were soon joined by their director.

"Right," said Victor with a sense of urgency. "You two know what we're doing?"

Phil nodded.

"Actually, I don't." Nesta raised her hand like a curious school pupil.

Victor squinted at her. "Don't I know you? Never mind — come with me." He walked her over to a set of stone steps and sat her down on the floor. "You'll be just here when Tankford comes out the front door." He signalled for one of his crew members and called out: "Can we get some more mud over here, please?!"

"Mud?" asked Nesta with a look of horror. She didn't have long to be curious and soon had a couple of people drenching her in buckets of cold dirt.

"That's it," said Victor. "I need more — *lots* more."

Darren was filming the entire spectacle from a safe distance, all whilst trying to keep a straight face. When the bombardment of mud flinging was over, a distraught Nesta wanted to curl up in a ball.

"Here's your line," said Victor, handing her a piece of paper. "You think you can manage that?"

Nesta nodded, wearily, praying for her onscreen debut to be over as soon as possible.

"Roll cameras! Ready — *Action!*"

There was a short pause, and the character of Tankford stepped out of his front door and took the first sips from a mug of tea. He walked outside of the property and was greeted by a woman on the street, who held out her hands and went down on one knee.

"Please, sir — spare some change!"

Tankford stared at her with his stern eyes. "Get away! Shoo! Away with you!" The man lifted up his mug and emptied the entire contents over the woman's head.

Darren almost gasped from behind the row of crew members, as Nesta clutched her wet face and sat back down.

The man beside her walked straight past and continued on his way."

"Cut!" Rory cried. The first AD turned to his director for a sign. "How was that?"

"Let's do that again," said Victor and could have sworn he heard a woman groan.

CHAPTER 25

"I have never been so humiliated in my life," said Nesta, as she made the long walk back to the hotel. In reality, it was a short distance but not when you were caked in mud and looking like a peasant from the dark ages.

"I thought you did a great job," said Darren, walking beside her through the busy street.

"A great job of being spat on by some man who thinks he's Oscar Wilde?"

"Didn't you say he gets killed off?"

Nesta smiled and revealed a row of teeth that the makeup artist had kindly blackened for her. "Yes, he gets murdered shortly after that scene. Thank goodness! I always love it when the victims are nasty pieces of work like that Tankford. Although, the man playing him seemed to be enjoying his role a little too much."

The sun was already beginning to set on yet another day on their Chester getaway, and Nesta began to wonder where the week had gone. She had experienced more in a few days than she had in the last few months and was determined to make the rest of her time in the city count.

"How about we go out tonight?" she asked once they turned onto Love Street.

The teenager turned to her. "Out? What do you mean — out?"

Nesta raised her arms into the air towards the tall building looking over them. "Out on the town, of course! We're in Chester! I think it's time we let our hair down."

"I think it's time you kept your hair on," said Darren. "The whole reason I came here was for some content. And I've barely shot anything. We're no closer to getting to the bottom of this Debbie Backes business — in fact, I think we're further away now than we were before!"

"I wouldn't be so sure about that." Nesta smiled again. "You might have been enjoying a nice, relaxing holiday so far, but I've been tinkering away, and I think I might be getting close."

"Seriously?" asked Darren. "How?!"

"I'll tell you over drinks." She turned serious for a moment. "Soft drinks for you, obviously."

Darren rolled his eyes. "Great. Sounds like we're going to have a crazy one."

As they approached the hotel's main entrance, Nesta saw a figure that made her want to run in the opposite direction. "Oh, God. Please hide me."

The confused teenager saw her cower behind him. "What's the matter?"

"Just don't let him see me like this," she snapped.

"Nesta? Nesta, is that you?"

Nesta poked her head out to see Malcolm walking towards them. The doorman witnessed her dishevelled appearance and didn't know what to say. "You look —"

"Horrible," said Nesta. "I know. It's a long story."

Malcolm nodded. "I just wanted to apologise for leaving so abruptly last night."

"Oh, you don't need to —"

"No, it was very rude of me." The man hung his head in shame. "If I'm honest, the food didn't sit well with me. I felt terrible."

Nesta saw the genuine remorse in his face and sighed. "I wanted to apologise, too. My mind and attention was all over the place. It had nothing to do with you. I think I need to learn to switch off sometimes."

The doorman chuckled. "Well, how about we try again?"

A surprised Nesta smiled at him. There was still hope after all, she thought. "You still want to have dinner? After the way I acted last night?"

"Of course," said Malcolm. "How about we do tomorrow night." He clutched his stomach. "Although, I might avoid the Beef Wellington this time."

They both chuckled, and the doorman tipped his hat before walking away.

Nesta had almost forgotten that Darren was still standing there and saw that he was cringing. "Did he really just ask me out on another date? Looking like — *this*?" She pointed to her muddy complexion and stained clothes.

"Yep," said Darren. "People in this city really are crazy. Or very short-sighted."

Nesta *whacked* him with her handbag, and they both headed inside.

AFTER SOAKING in a hot bath for well over an hour, Nesta was finally back to her old, clean self. Even Darren had made an effort to scrub up a little, by gelling up his hair and shaving off the thin layer of fluff that he liked to call stubble. If it was a night on the town that they were about to have, then he wanted to be ready. After all, this was not an evening at the *Pizzeria* in Bala they were talking about.

"Not bad," said Nesta, as he stepped out of the bathroom. "I didn't even know you owned a shirt." The word "shirt" had been very generous, but she didn't want to knock the young man's confidence.

The two companions headed out into the streets of Chester like two people walking down the Las Vegas strip.

Darren had been quite surprised at Nesta's insistence of heading out so late, and she had recommended a bar called *The Timeless Hour*, which turned out to be a lot more trendy than he had expected. It reminded him of somewhere he would have hoped to find on a long road trip down Route 66 with its neon signs behind the bar and hard rock music playing on the jukebox.

"Where did you hear about this place?" he asked, as they both enjoyed their beverages in the corner of the lively bar.

"You know me," said Nesta. "I'm always in the know when it comes to the cool places." She checked her watch. Not long now, she thought.

"So what makes you think that you're so close to solving this Debbie Backes business?" Darren asked, sipping on his *Coke*.

"Well, one of the most important factors in a murder like this is motive. Now, we all know few people actually *liked* Debbie Backes, but if everyone killed someone because they didn't like someone, there'd hardly be anyone left."

Darren nodded. He couldn't argue with that. "I'd definitely be in trouble."

Nesta nodded. She couldn't argue with that, either. "So, I've been thinking — there was a plate of half-eaten food on the floor in that room. That steak knife she was killed with was taken from the plate, which means that whoever killed her hadn't necessarily entered the room with the intention of stabbing her in the chest. Which brings us to another important factor — opportunity. The killer took the opportunity to kill her in the moment. The original intention of entering that room was not to murder, but for something else. The shower was still running, so Debbie obviously didn't let the killer in, or she would have stopped the water. And she wouldn't have heard the *knock* anyway whilst being in the shower. Her hair was still wet. Why else would a person sneak into someone's room whilst they were having a shower?"

Darren thought about it. "Peeping Tom?"

Nesta frowned. "Is that really where your mind goes?"

The teenager shuddered. "Maybe not with Debbie Backes."

"They were obviously trying to steal something. And to get into the room, they needed a keycard."

"*They?*"

The doors to the bar burst open, and Nesta and Darren turned around to see a group of familiar faces enter with laughs and cries.

"Right on time," Nesta muttered.

The Ten O'Clock Crew headed to their usual table in the centre of the room and consisted of; Frida, the receptionist; Leigh and Amy, the waiting staff; Jack, the pot washer; Julian, the concierge.

A suspicious Darren turned to study Nesta's smiling face. "Did you know they were going to be here?"

"Of course," said Nesta. "It's Thursday."

The barman headed over to the group's table with a tray of beers, and Nesta was soon spotted by the gang's apparent ringleader.

"Nesta?!" Frida called. She gave her a frantic wave. "Come join us!"

Nesta and Darren were soon sharing a table with a group of hotel staff who couldn't wait to blow off some steam. They all raised up their drinks with a "Cheers!", and the heavy drinking began.

"So this is a regular thing?" Darren asked. He was already on his third *Coke* and was beginning to feel sick from all the sugar.

"Absoluetly," said Frida. "The original *Ten O'Clock Crew!*" She raised up her fist and the others joined in. "All for one, and one for all! Well, not everyone. We're still missing a couple of people."

"I believe Billy was one of your honorary members," said Nesta with a cheeky smile.

The mention of the head chef's name caused Frida to groan in disgust. "Yeah, we don't need that traitor anymore. You're either in or you're out."

Nesta waited patiently for the beer to flow, and, before long, the entire crew were a few drinks deep into their drinking session.

"So what else does your little group get up to when you're not here?" Nesta asked. "Apart from working at the hotel, of course."

Frida looked over at her fellow comrades, and they all smiled at each other. "Oh, we get up to all sorts." Her eyes were now red from the alcohol, and she was swaying in her chair. "What do we reckon, guys? Shall we tell her about our last little shenanigans?"

"Is that a good idea?" asked Julian, who was now slumped down against his large forearms.

"She can be trusted," said Frida. "We can make these two honorary members!" She laughed. "Besides, it's not like our little heist actually worked. But it's a funny story."

"Heist?" Darren asked. "You mean, like a bank heist?"

Frida cackled and slammed the table. "Sure! Like a bank heist. We're like Jesse James or Butch Cassidy."

"More like Robin Hood and his merry men," said Leigh. "Steal from the rich and give to the poor."

"With us lot being the poor!" Jack cried. The others laughed.

Frida looked around to check if anyone was listening and leant forward towards Nesta. "This is our little secret. It doesn't go out of this circle."

Nesta smiled. "Consider me your Maid Marian."

The group laughed again.

"Well —" Frida was about to tell her tale, when the front door opened again.

"Where the hell have you been?" asked Jack, as a sheepish Henry made his way inside.

"Henry?" Nesta asked, watching the young porter take a seat. "You're telling me that *you're* part of this crew?"

A confused Henry looked around at his fellow colleagues. "*What* crew?"

The group howled with laughter.

"That a boy!" Leigh cried. "Young Henry's still in his probation phase." He placed an arm around him. "Aren't you, lad?"

Frida chucked a toothpick at the waiter's forehead. "Leave him alone! He's more trustworthy than you are!"

Leigh released his grip and frowned. "Hey, at least I didn't screw up my role!"

"I didn't screw up," Henry snapped.

"Screw up what?" asked Darren. "The heist?"

The group gave each other a knowing glance.

"Does your uncle know that you're out this late?" Nesta asked, making Henry blush, as her question amused his friends even further.

"I don't need his permission to do anything," Henry snapped. "I'm not a child. I work at this hotel, too."

"You tell her," Jack cried, patting the porter on the back.

Nesta shook her head in disappointment and turned back to Frida. "Please feel free to continue your story."

Frida was more than happy to oblige. "So, there's this necklace…"

"The *Backes Diamond*?" Nesta asked.

The surprised group roared with surprise.

"She's not daft, this woman, is she?" asked Julian.

"I told you," said Frida. "She's as sharp as the rest of us." She looked down at her beer, and her eyes twinkled as though the necklace was resting in the bottom of the glass. "I remember when that actor first arrived at the hotel. I asked her if she needed a safe for the item around her neck, and she showed it to me. She said that it never left her neck, which I thought was pretty stupid, to be honest. Then I found out how much it was worth…" She rubbed her fingers together. "It was too good of an opportunity to miss. But I needed a proper plan. And I couldn't do it alone." She looked up at her colleagues. "We would all have a part to play, and we would all have a cut. First, we had to not make it look like a robbery. Debbie had to seem crazy enough that she could have lost it anywhere. So we went about making her look as mad as a hatter."

"We didn't have to try *too* hard," said Leigh.

"But it had to be subtle," Frida continued. "So, we began playing tricks on her."

"Tricks?" asked Nesta. "You mean pranks? Like leaving a severed hand on her pillow?" She looked over at Leigh, who struggled to keep a straight face.

"Exactly!" Frida chuckled. "Harmless little pranks that slowly made her feel like she was losing her mind."

"Don't forget the drinks," said Jack with a snigger.

"Yes," said Frida. "We all took turns adding various things to her drinks and food."

"Things?" asked Nesta.

"Different kinds of hallucinogens to affect her senses. It got pretty trippy for her after a while. We may have over done it. She would have had some crazy dreams. And it worked like a charm. She was driving the hotel management nuts. They thought she was bonkers."

"And so wouldn't have been surprised if she'd lost her necklace," said Nesta. She tried not to show her extreme disapproval.

"Exactly!"

"So where did the peanut powder come in?" asked Darren. "Last time I checked, peanuts don't make you hallucinate."

"Ah," said Frida. "That was part of the heist itself." She prepared for her favourite part of the plan. "We knew our best chance of getting the necklace was when she was tucked up in bed. But we needed some control on when that would happen, and an excuse for her to head to bed early. Food poisoning was too slow. We needed something simple that would instantly make her ill and distract everyone from what we were about to do. That's when I found out about the peanut allergy."

"You know a peanut allergy can kill a person?" asked Nesta.

Frida shrugged. "The plan was only to sprinkle the tiniest bit. Only Amy, here, went overboard."

The waitress frowned. "I was under a lot of pressure! And my hand was shaking."

"Luckily," Frida continued. "Debbie recovered after her injection, and she ended up being taken to bed. So that still worked for us. The next phase involved a power cut and a grease man."

"*Grease* man?" asked Darren.

"Like the acrobat from *Ocean's Eleven*," said Julian. "Someone who can hide in small places."

"Right," said Frida. "We needed someone small enough to hide underneath Debbie's bed before she got there and wait until she was dead asleep. And we knew the perfect man for the job." She turned to look at Henry. The porter nodded, much to Nesta's horror. "Our tech man would create a short powercut at exactly eleven past the hour, every hour."

"That's another *Ocean's Eleven* nod," said Julian, proudly. "That's why I chose eleven-past to turn off the power."

Frida rolled her eyes. "Yes, thank you for that, Julian. So, our friend Henry just had to check his watch, and if he could hear that Debbie was asleep at those times, he could be safe that it would be pitch black in that room to do his thing."

"Which was what exactly?" asked Nesta.

"Get the necklace," said Henry, very matter-of-factly.

"I supplied him with the room card," said Frida. " And he just had to get that necklace from around Debbie's neck."

"It should have been so easy," Leigh muttered.

"Well it wasn't," Henry snapped. "The first time, I couldn't get the thing off in time before the power came back on."

"Turns out Debbie liked to sleep with all her lamps on," said Frida.

"Then the second time I tried," Henry continued, "she woke up and saw me."

"What did she do?" asked Nesta.

"She just screamed. So I legged it out of there. I thought for certain I was busted."

Frida sniggered. "The next morning, Debbie had complained to someone that she dreamt about seeing a dragon by her bed. Turns out all those hallucinogens had really wrecked her sleep."

"So I was off the hook," said Henry. "The plan was for me to try again the next night. But she was already dead by then."

"Someone had got there first," said Frida with a frown. "But their methods were far more ruthless than ours."

"We were *this* close," said Julian, holding up his fingers. "Now some other person's rich."

The table went silent, as the *The Ten O'Clock Crew* commiserated their failed heist with a few more sips of beer.

"Oh, well." Leigh sighed. "At least we have our freedom. We could have succeeded and then all got sent to prison."

"You call working at that hotel *freedom*?" asked Jack.

Nesta and Darren finished their drinks and bid the crew a farewell. As they approached the exit, the teenager whispered in her ear: "Before we go…" He pointed back towards the hotel workers. "Take a look at their shoes. *All* of them."

A confused Nesta turned back to look underneath their table. It took her a moment, but she soon realised what Darren had discovered.

CHAPTER 26

Nesta stared into her menu, her eyes glazing over the selection of starters. Her mind was still preoccupied with the meeting at *The Timeless Hour*. Frida's heist may not have gone to plan, but someone out there was now in possession of Debbie's necklace, and it had cost the woman her life.

She gazed around the dining hall and saw various members of the cast and crew. Her thoughts turned to the hotel porter and his failed attempt. Something did not seem right, and she feared the worst. To make matters even worse, she was now sitting opposite the uncle and guardian of the person she suspected of killing Debbie Backes.

"Are you alright?" asked Malcolm. The doorman was sitting opposite her again with his menu at the ready. Once again, his dinner date had seemed distant.

Nesta looked up with a concerned expression. "I'm sorry, Malcolm. I keep doing this to you."

Malcolm chuckled. "You don't need to apologise. Is it something you want to talk about? Something you want to share? Always good to get it off your chest."

"I don't think this is something you want to hear," said Nesta.

The doorman looked confused. "Oh, I see." He placed his menu down and sighed. "You don't need to worry about hurting my feelings. I get it. I'm old enough to handle the truth. I shouldn't have been so pushy."

Nesta's eyes widened, as she realised what he was implying. "Oh, no! I'm not talking about you and me. I mean — not that you and I are necessarily a —" She stopped herself and took a deep breath. "This is about Henry."

"Henry?" Now the man was even more confused. "What *about* Henry?"

"Have you noticed that he's been acting a little strange, lately?"

Malcolm chuckled. "The man is practically still a teenager. And they're always strange."

Nesta thought about Darren and nodded. "Yes, but... have you noticed him being a little *on edge*? Has he seemed worried about something?"

The man sighed and tried to think. "Well, he hasn't been at home as much, I suppose. Sometimes he gets back quite late. But we're a strange house like that. Both of us work strange hours, and we're always in and out."

Nesta glanced down at the knife on her table. Her stomach went tense, as she tried to pluck up the courage to tell him what she was really thinking. "I don't know how to tell you this, Malcolm. But I wanted to say something before I go to the police."

"The police?" Malcolm's mouth began to droop open in disbelief, and he leant forward. "Nesta, what's going on? You need to tell me."

"I think Henry may have killed Debbie Backes." She paused to take a breath. "He was involved with this group who were trying to steal her necklace, a group of staff members from the hotel. I didn't want to believe it — honestly, I didn't — but when I heard that he was the last person in possession of the spare room key, it seemed like the only possible solution." She waited for a response, but the doorman remained quiet, seemingly in shock. "He seemed frustrated that he'd failed to get the necklace, and, so, a second attempt was inevitably on the cards whilst he still had the key. The steak knife from Debbie's meal implied that there was a scuffle after he tried to sneak into her room whilst she was taking a shower. The shower was still running, so she must have jumped out and grabbed her dressing gown. Then, there was the woman that was spotted fleeing from the room. Darren told me that the witness had seen this person wearing red trainers, which seemed like an odd choice. I hadn't seen Henry's casual shoes until last night. They were red trainers." Malcolm looked as though he was going to sink through the base of his chair. "I saw the dress and wig a few days before when I was in her room. It was the costume that Debbie wore to play her character in *Steeping Road*. Henry must have put it on to escape the room without anyone seeing his face. I'm really sorry, Malcolm. I really am. But I wanted to be the one to tell you."

The doorman stared at her, as though she was trying to force a spear through his chest. "You don't need to be sorry. I appreciate your honesty."

Nesta could sense his change in tone and realised that whatever relationship they *could* have had together was never going to happen now. There was nothing like a person telling you that your loved one is a killer to sabotage any hint of romance.

"You understand that we're going to have to tell the police?" she asked. "We don't know how he's going to react if we confront him."

Malcolm leant forward across the table and looked her in the eye. "We're not going to the police."

"But, he's —"

"Henry didn't kill Debbie Backes. I'm certain of it."

Nesta's heart sank. He didn't believe her, she thought. "How can you be so certain?"

"Because I'm the one who killed her."

Nesta could no longer hear the ambience of the dining hall. Any background noise had now faded into a muffled hum, as she stared at Malcolm's serious face. The blood had rushed from her cheeks, and her muscles were trembling.

"Henry came to me the morning after this so-called heist," Malcolm said. "The lad was in bits. He was certain that Debbie had seen him in her room, and he was terrified that she was going to tell the police. He told me everything about this elaborate plan that Frida and her minions had concocted. It all sounded ridiculous. I told him to give me the key card and that everything would be fine. When it turned out that Debbie hadn't remembered seeing Henry at all, we knew he was in the clear. That's when I suggested a plan of our own."

"*Why*, Malcolm?" Nesta shook her head in disappointment. "Why, after all these years of working here would you want to risk everything?"

"Risk what?" Malcolm snapped. He tried to calm himself down. "I've dedicated my life to this hotel. I've done everything that's been asked of me. Now, I'm on the verge of retirement, and I barely have a penny to my name. I never took out a mortgage, always paid my rent, I barely put anything into my pension until recently. And I was practically a single parent. This was a chance to get what I deserved." His face lit up for a moment. "I wasn't going to let a bunch of lazy, disrespectful youngsters have the opportunity. So, I told Henry to keep this to himself. He could tell his clock crew — or whatever they're called — that he'd failed again. It was all quite simple really. To try and get hold of a necklace that a person never took off — even for bed — you had to wait for the one time she took *everything* off."

Nesta nodded. "The shower."

"Exactly," said Malcolm. "Debbie was known for her early evening requests. A snack before her shower and a gin and tonic for after. She was very particular about it. And, like clockwork, she did the same thing the day I went up to her room. I could hear the shower running from outside her door. I searched the room, but there was no sign of the necklace. So, I headed to the bathroom. There was so much steam that I couldn't see a thing, and, then, there it was." His eyes widened. "The necklace was lying there beside the sink, and Debbie was hidden behind the shower curtain. I knew I didn't have long, and, as I reached to grab the necklace, I knocked over an empty wineglass. The next thing I know, Debbie was screaming. Stupidly, I tried to calm her down and told her it was just me delivering some room service. She didn't buy that, obviously, and grabbed her dressing gown. When she realised that the necklace was missing, she chased me out into the bedroom. I insisted that I didn't know what she was talking about, that it was all a misunderstanding. That's when she threatened me..." Malcolm's eyes darkened. "She said that if I didn't hand back the necklace, I'd have the police to deal with. Either way, even if I *did* hand it back, I could kiss my career and reputation goodbye. I'd be reported to the hotel owners and sacked by the next day. She would do everything in her power to ruin me and told me how my entire job was a joke — that anyone who opened doors for a living should be embarrassed." The man took a deep breath, and his hands were trembling. "Something about that last insult touched a nerve. I could suddenly hear my father again. All these years that I'd spent trying to prove him wrong, trying to do the best job I could, with dignity and honour — all that would have been for nothing thanks to this stupid woman and her precious necklace. I looked over and saw the steak knife lying on a plate of food and grabbed it. I was just trying to scare her at first and told her to shut up. Instead, she came running at me, crying out for her necklace." The man took a hard gulp. "The next thing I remember, that steak knife was buried into her chest."

Nesta closed her eyes. It saddened her that a life could be taken so easily and so carelessly.

"I got out of there so quickly," Malcolm continued, "I didn't even bother to close the door. Which, considering my profession, is pretty ironic, I suppose. A minute or so after I'd left the room, Henry came to look for me. The door was still open, and he went in and found her. You were right about the dress. He heard people coming and tried to cover himself up to get away."

Nesta normally enjoyed being right but not when it came to something like this. "You know what you need to do now," she said.

Malcolm saw her expression and shook his head. "I can't. Surely, Nesta, you can understand. That woman was a nasty, vile piece of work. I'm not ruining the rest of my life — and Henry's — because of *her*."

"Then I'll have to tell them for you," said Nesta.

The doorman seemed bitterly disappointed. He had grown to like this woman and couldn't bear the thought of her turning him in. "You don't have any proof."

"We found the clothes that Henry was wearing. Then there's the fingerprints on the keycard you would have had returned. Not to mention the amount of DNA you must have left in the room. It was probably only a matter of time." She reached into her handbag and pulled out her mobile phone.

Malcolm's face dropped. "You've been recording this?"

Nesta nodded, and it pained her to admit it. "I'm not normally very good with technology. But, luckily, my friend has taught me well when it comes to sound recording. Did you know that you can even send voice messages these days? Incredible. Some people even send whole video recordings, apparently. I told him that, back in our day, we used a good-old-fashioned answering machine. Same thing as far as I'm concerned."

The doorman stared at her. His heart was broken, as was hers. "Well," he said. "I guess that's it, then."

"Yes," said Nesta with a sigh. "I suppose it is."

"If you change your mind," said Malcolm, "about going to the police, I mean... you know where to find me." The weary doorman stood up and delivered his last words to her: "It's been a pleasure, Nesta. It really has. I'm sorry it had to end this way."

Nesta nodded and watched the man walk away. "Me too, Malcolm."

CHAPTER 27

The final day of shooting for opera-singer-turned-actor Phil Wogan took place in a cemetery on the east side of the city. It was also the last day of Nesta and Darren's week in Chester, and what better way to spend it than to witness the death scene of a character called Tankford. Nesta had been looking forward to this scene ever since her mucky onscreen debut, and she couldn't wait to see the Victorian gentleman get his just desserts.

"So, who killed him?" asked Darren, as they both stood among the gravestones, watching an uncomfortable Phil being bloodied-up whilst lying on the ground.

"You'll have to watch the film," said Nesta. "Or read the book."

An impatient Darren sighed. "Imagine trying to catch a serial killer. At least the murders we've been dealing with have only involved one victim."

Nesta had to pause and think for a moment. "I think, technically, there were two victims in Talacre. But a few decades apart. Still, that wasn't really a serial killer situation."

Darren shrugged. "Hopefully we never have to come across one of *those*."

"Apparently," said Nesta, "most serial killers pick their victims at random. So, it's even harder."

"Great content for the channel, though."

The sun was already beginning to set, and the director was running around, stressed out of his mind. "If we don't shoot soon, we're going to miss magic hour!"

"What's magic hour?" Nesta whispered.

"It's the time of day when the light is perfect for filming," said Darren. "Just before sunset, basically."

Nesta nodded and looked out at the cemetery with its Chester backdrop. She found it strange how a yard so full of death could also possess a certain beauty in the right light.

"I need to do this more often," she said.

"Do — what?" Darren gave her a strange look. "Hang out in graveyards?"

"No, silly. I mean visit more places. I've enjoyed Chester. It's made me realise that you don't even need to go that far for a change in scenery. Take North Wales, for instance. There's so many places: Pwllheli, Barmouth, Anglesey, Conwy, Ruthin..." Nesta sighed. "So many beautiful locations, and so little time."

"I don't know what you're complaining about," said Darren. "You've got *loads* of time on your hands."

"Speak for yourself," Nesta snapped.

"Let's just hope you come across another murder soon." Darren lifted up his phone and began inspecting his latest channel views and likes. "We're going to need more content if we want to build up the subscribers."

Nesta smiled. "Oh, don't you worry about that. If there's one thing I'm learning in my retirement, it's that death and murder are only around the corner. There's still plenty of lying, cheating and deceiving left to go around — even in North Wales. It's a strange world out there. People are complicated creatures, and I'm sure we won't have to wait too long. Unlike the movies, you can't just call out the word *'cut'* and expect the world to stop."

She looked down at the corpse of Tankford lying amongst the gravestones. Bella Marsh was standing in position above him with her onscreen assistant, Bamber, by her side. The two fictional sleuths were about to find their latest murder victim, and all that was left to be said was a single word: *"Action!"*

ABOUT THE AUTHOR

We hope you enjoyed this book. Reviews are extremely important for new authors, so please do feel free to write a short review on the book's Amazon page.

Whilst you're waiting for Book 5 in this new series, why not try the first book in another P. L Handley murder mystery series:

The Murder Ledger
By P. L. Handley
Available on Amazon

If you'd like to read more books in this new series, you can join the P. L. Handley e-mail newsletter and receive all the latest news on future releases.

Subscribe to the e-mailing list by visiting the official P. L. Handley website at: www.plhandley.com

THE MURDER LEDGER

When an elderly lottery winner goes missing in a small, rural town, it's up to a tenacious, local reporter to solve the case. Aided by a curious accountant with a methodical brain, Rhiannon must use her new (and unlikely) partnership to uncover a series of shocking secrets. Click the image below to view on Amazon.

www.plhandley.com